TE[...]

VOL[...]

FREDERIC RAPHAEL
RICHARD BURNS
DONNA TARTT
DEBORAH MOGGACH
JULIA O' FAOLAIN
BERYL BAINBRIDGE
JOYCE CAROL OATES
STEVE DIXON
JULIE BURCHILL
CLARE BOYLAN
MICHAEL CARSON
MOY McCRORY
CAROLINE FORBES
JONATHAN TREITEL
MARTYN READ
FAY WELDON
CARL TIGHE
ALAN BEARD
NIGEL WILLIAMS
MAURICE LEITCH

Duncan Minshull

TELLING STORIES

Introduction and Compilation
copyright © 1994, Duncan Minshull
For Copyright on individual stories see
page 221

First published in Great Britain in
1994 by Sceptre Books

A Sceptre Original

Sceptre is an Imprint of Hodder
and Stoughton Ltd, a division
of Hodder Headline PLC

British Library C.I.P.
Telling Stories. – Vol. 3: Best of
BBC Radio's Recent Short Fiction
   I. Minshull, Duncan
823.01080914 [FS]

ISBN 0 340-59794-1

Printed and bound in Great Britain for
Hodder and Stoughton Paperbacks, a
division of Hodder and Stoughton Ltd,
a division of Hodder Headline plc, 338
Euston Road, London NW1 3BH by
Cox & Wyman Typeset by Hewer Text
Composition Services, Edinburgh.

CONTENTS

INTRODUCTION

Welcome to the radio story in print. For the third year running, a selection of twenty you may have first encountered on Radio 4's *Short Story* programme or on Radio 3 before and after various evening concerts. Once again we have kept to a policy of freshness, with the following published for the first time in book form.

Freshness and, I hope, variety. In the last twelve months BBC Radio has broadcast nearly two hundred new stories on the two networks, either commissioned pieces or the best of the unsolicited. With the magazine and book trades only fitfully supporting the genre, it is fair to say that short fiction is now written to be heard as much as it was ever conceived to be read on the page – no excuses, then, not to reflect the greatest mix in author and subject matter.

The contributors themselves, as is the habit, fall into one of three categories. Out in force are the experts such as Frederic Raphael, Clare Boylan, Joyce Carol Oates; the newcomers are here – Caroline Forbes, Alan Beard, Steve Dixon; and there are novelists like Nigel Williams and Donna Tartt who make up the newly converted: they established themselves writing long and for the first time find their voices in a shorter form. The late Richard Burns should be added to this group.

And writing for radio is writing very short; it never ceases to surprise how whole worlds can be created in less than three thousand words. Less in this case is definitely more. I would like to think that a single-voice reading, often scheduled between more lavishly produced programmes, can in its own way and just as effectively take the listener to places new and unexplored. And where do we go to this year? Well, prepare ahead for storms in Miami, for bitter-sweet moments in a nuts and bolts factory; we observe the ghoulish desires of a centenarian vicar and see Amsterdam through the eyes of a *Blind Date* winner. Then there are dubious games at the Wimbledon Heights Tennis Club, Southfields.

Indeed, it's more than appropriate to borrow from the title of Michael Carson's tale; in the pages ahead we are unashamedly All Over the Place.

Good reading!

Duncan Minshull
Short Story Editor, BBC Radio

THE WIFE OF MY FRIEND

Frederic Raphael

Frederic Raphael was born in Chicago in 1931, and educated at Charterhouse and St John's College, Cambridge. He has published novels and many short stories. His most recent novel is *A Double Life*. His new collection of short stories will be published by Orion later this year. He lives in France.

THE WIFE OF MY FRIEND was first broadcast on Radio 3, read by the author.

THE WIFE OF MY FRIEND

The first time we went to the island, the steamer left Piraeus in the evening and arrived at three in the morning. In the early spring there were few other passengers. The *Despina* – the Greek word for mistress – had once been a channel steamer; at the head of the stairs, an embossed steel plate declared its origins on Tyneside. First-class passengers could rent tight, stuffy cabins. Our two children fell asleep innocently enough but, knowing that I should be roused in a few hours, I left Sylvia with them and went on deck. Coastal lights swung up and down as though the horizon were a line strung with tiny lanterns.

I had brought a volume of Sophocles with me, like homework I should have finished years before. I was leaning against the rail, under a lamp, when a man who was neither tall nor short, neither thin nor fat, but both commanding and solid, came out of the saloon and lit a cigarette.

Was I holding my book in order that he could see what a serious Hellenist I was? I know only that I pretended to be surprised when I heard him say, 'Sophoklis!' He might have been recognising me rather than my text. Although it was a relief to discover that Vassili spoke much better English than I ever would Greek, our friendship was stranded from the beginning on an island where neither of us could express ourselves without a certain fear either of being misunderstood or of saying the wrong thing.

Hindsight may have freighted that first meeting with an excess of significance; but even after a quarter of a century I can recall the look which he gave to two army officers as they stepped out of the saloon to go to their cabins, the major with worry beads deferring to the colonel without. They were accompanied on their lurching way by a Greek Orthodox priest, whose hieratic beard and cylindrical hat seemed to have been borrowed from Byzantium.

'Picturesque, do you think?' said Vassili.

I said, 'The traveller sees as scenery what others experience as power.'

He came closer and stood calmly on the pitching deck. 'How long will you stay?'

'As long as we can afford it.'

'Everyone can afford Greece,' Vassili replied. 'Greece is easy to buy. *Sigaretta?*' It sounded more like an order than an offer. Even before he told me that he had been a sea captain, he gave an impression of expecting to be obeyed. 'You don't even have to buy it; you can just shake it sometimes. Greece, I mean.'

'Then *kapneezo*,' I said, glad to prove how diligently I had studied my phrasebook. 'I don't smoke.'

'We always know precisely what we don't do. We never know exactly what we will, or might.'

A beautiful woman with very white teeth and frowning black brows leaned out round the door of the saloon. Because her head alone was visible, with its crown of raven hair, she reminded me of some ancient coin, artfully lit to sharpen its profile. She had gleaming dark eyes and the classic Greek nose so few Greeks have. Her skin was almost chalky, though her lips were brightly reddened. She said, 'Vassili? *To cafe!*'

'*Erchome, erchome.*' He looked at me with the same hint of irony as before. 'You want to have a coffee?'

'Your wife?'

He said, 'The wife of my friend.'

A few hours later, the steward called the name of the island which had been recommended to us for its unspoiled remoteness. At first there was nothing to be seen, but then the *Despina* rounded a headland and a lighthouse twitched its blind welcome. Stunned with surprise at being woken, our children gazed out as we surged past the bright rocks and seemed to enter a new pit of blackness. After a few moments, I pointed to a fluctuating red glow coming towards the *Despina*'s side. The anchor rattled and fell into the harbour. The raspberry of light came from the cigarette of one of the men rowing out to meet us.

12

THE WIFE OF MY FRIEND

The harbour had no jetty. We were already going down the unsteady ladder when Vassili and the other disembarking passengers came on deck. I watched anxiously as my children and my wife and my typewriter were received into the lurching boat. Vassili allowed the beautiful woman and another, less beautiful, to precede him. He and his friend came last.

Vassili's wife was called Anna. The beautiful woman was introduced to us, as other travellers came down with their luggage; including two goats and some chickens heartlessly immobilised with tightly bound claws. Her name was Elektra. Her husband, Loukas, was a journalist, thin and unsmiling, almost bald, with thick spectacles which required him to tilt his head back in order to bring you into focus. He could give you his attention only by backing away.

Vassili and Anna had a place on the island to which, as we parted, he invited us. 'Ask for Pavlides' house.'

I was anxious to find a cottage, where I should be able to work and where Sylvia and the children could feel at home. At a distance, I had been sure that we should have no problem. Now, marooned on the island, I felt like Sisyphus, doomed forever to roll the stone of family responsibility. Having told myself that I would not seek Vassili's help, I soon went to the turreted house overlooking the harbour and explained the problem. Vassili knew of a little cottage in the *campo* with two rooms and a kitchen. It was owned by a peasant who would think he was cheating us for two pounds a week. There was a well, but no electricity. The lavatory was a hut on the edge of a field with a hole in the floor. A grape vine covered the terrace. There was a table for the typewriter. The children had portable beds we had brought from England; Niko could offer only a rusty bed-frame and a straw mattress which rested on planks. What more could one want?

Vassili asked us to eat with them on the evening before they went back to Athens. Their maid, Flora, came to listen for the children. Vassili's wife, Anna, cooked lobster and we drank jugs of harsh *retsina*. Loukas talked politics. His jargon was more savage than his tone; his contempt for the royal family and for the 'classic right-wing' was uttered almost tenderly. He thought the boy-king, whom he called 'the yachtsman', a fool who had been dominated by his German mother. While the beautiful Elektra helped Anna with the dinner, she told Sylvia that she and Loukas had two children, who were staying in Athens with her mother. Vassili and Anna, who owned two carpet shops on Ermou Street, had three daughters. Our new friends' lives were not as neat as envy would wish.

A year later, the Colonels' tanks clanked into Athens. Loukas was arrested; his articles had lashed them with unforgivable satires. Advised to go into hiding, he elected to wait in open scorn for their vengeance. In the sixties, fortunes changed very swiftly. The book I wrote on the island, watched by our landlord, Nikos, who had never before seen a typewriter, was sold to the movies. I was hired to write the screenplay and we were able to buy a house in Chelsea. Loukas was in jail.

In the early months of the Colonels' regime, the new tyrants were torn between ruthlessness at home and making a good impression abroad. One day the telephone rang in Seymour Walk. It was Vassili: 'A friend of mine will come to your house in a few days. Please give him whatever he asks. I will repay it when I see you.'

The friend was Loukas. He was alone in London. The Colonels had expelled him from Greece, but they had refused exit visas to Elektra and their children. 'I am muzzled, you see: I am forbidden to write and I am forbidden to speak. Otherwise, I am free!' His voice carried something of Vassili's accusing wryness. 'I need five hundred pounds.'

As we walked to the bank, I asked how his wife and children would cope. He smiled, as if it were the natural response to pain. 'Vassili will look after them. Vassili is very fond of Elektra.' Did he scan me for the reaction I was careful not to have? I had never forgotten how Elektra had looked at Vassili, and he at her, when I first met them. It was not by chance that I had assumed her his wife. How could the dumpy, competent Anna satisfy a beached corsair like Vassili?

During that busy, inane time in London when I wrote movies and grew my hair and appeared on television and tried, as it were, to eat ten meals a day (most of them at Franco and Mario's), I also took Greek lessons from Loukas. I hoped for news from the Athens underground, perhaps even to be enrolled in its courier service, but I discovered Loukas to be a dry teacher. When he gave me grammatical rules to learn and homework to do, I proved a more reliable paymaster than I was student. I admired Loukas and I was sorry for him in his loneliness, but I could not warm to him.

When Vassili rang me to ask when we were coming to Greece, I said that my friends thought that we should boycott the Fascist regime.

He said, 'Come. Show your contempt for them. They have hijacked Greece. Besides –' and now I could imagine the curl of his lip, the grey humour in his eyes '– besides, you have credit here.'

We did not go until the following summer. We had dinner with Vassili and Anna in Kifissia. We went to their elegant shop and admired the hand-woven carpets from Volos. He repaid the money I had advanced to Loukas. When I thanked him, he said, 'Why do you thank me? Did you not expect to see it again?'

I asked after Elektra. 'You will see her,' he said. 'She is on the island. I am coming next week.'

Aware that Anna was watching me, I said, 'How is she managing?'

'She has a job. She is also quite clever, you know.' The way he said 'also' was the only allusion I ever heard him make to the beauty of the woman I assumed him to love.

Elektra had the capacity, shared by many beautiful women, to behave modestly, as if no one was looking at her. On the island, she wore no make-up, a black skirt and a collarless cotton shirt, of the kind they called '*choriatiko*', as made in the village. While we were at the cottage, our children played with hers, but not often, and not easily: little Pavlo was a ruffian.

When Vassili came from Athens, he brought us two rugs which we had admired. With English squeamishness, I had not cared to ask their price. I tried to refuse what was now a gift. 'Among Greeks,' Vassili said, 'we accept what our friends give us.'

15

Did I somehow convey my feeling that it was not right that he should be with the wife of a man who was in exile? I took refuge in work. Sylvia spent the mornings on the beach, while I filled the quota required to satisfy my statistical muse. Vassili and Elektra would sometimes join her, with Dmitra and the meaty little Pavlo.

When the boat came in, with fresh vegetables from Naxos, I went up to the village to do some shopping and saw Vassili in Kosta's cafe. He was reading one of the newspapers which were still allowed to publish. He held the folded front page towards me, indicating where I should read. I frowned at the text as I once did at Greek Unseen examination papers. The gist was that the Colonels' Greece was regarded as a much more reliable ally by the Americans and the English. 'And you are the friends of liberty,' Vassili said. 'The countrymen of Lord Byron!'

'They kicked Byron out like your people did Loukas.'

'My people? Do you call that scum mine?' He had turned so that his words could carry across the square, to where the village priest and the police chief could hear him. 'Your wife doesn't approve of me. She thinks me . . . sarcastic.'

'She's extremely grateful to you,' I said. 'Me too. The carpets are wonderful. Just what the cottage needed.'

'I want no gratitude for carpets. She thinks I have no shame. Why are you red in the face?'

'Because it's hot.'

'What do you think of Elektra and me?'

'I don't think anything.'

'A writer who does not think,' Vassili said, 'can only be English!'

'All right then, I think she's very beautiful and that you are a man who does what he wants to do.'

'And sells carpets? You insult me! I gave up the sea for my wife. I carry a fan now, like Lord Byron. Do you think I am sleeping with Elektra? What will you say to Loukas? What will you *not* say? The only interesting thing about Englishmen is what they hide. For your information, I have not *touched* Elektra – I have literally not touched Elektra – since Loukas was arrested. Do you believe me?'

'Yes. I believe you.'

'Why? Because I tell you to?'

'Because it combines honour and perversity.'

'Thank you,' Vassili said. 'For your first intelligent words.'

After we flew back to England, I wrote to thank him for the carpets, one of which we took back to Chelsea. Loukas smiled when he saw it; his smile, like Vassili's, was more expressive than any English smile because it made no pretence of amusement. When I told Loukas how well his wife looked and how nicely his children had played with ours, he did not press for details, but began an analysis of the king's latest ineptitude. He seemed more intimately concerned with public than with private events. He had found a job in a Greek bookshop and had a busier social life. I continued to give him money, but our regular lessons ceased.

The next time we went to the island, Vassili's house was shuttered and empty. Sylvia was not sorry; I said that I wasn't. In Athens, on the way home, I went to the big shop, but to my disappointed relief he was not there. Anna looked fatter and she was suddenly grey; I suppose she has ceased to dye her hair. I asked how Vassili was and she said, 'How is he? He is a man who does what he chooses to do. Now he wants to buy a ship.'

Whenever I saw Loukas, which was rarely, since I had a film shooting in France, I expected to hear that Vassili had been arrested, but nothing like that happened. What did happen was more prosaic: the next time we were in Athens, I went to Ermou Street and found that the big shop was closed and padlocked. Vassili was in the smaller one, which was mostly basement. 'Ah,' he said, 'the occasional tourist!'

I had the impression that things were not good, but his pride was, if anything, more obvious. I told him that Loukas now had a job and that I wanted to regard the additional money he had had from me as a bonus for his teaching me Greek.

Vassili said, 'If he is that good, why are we speaking English? Let us speak Greek.' He began to do so, at speed. His flattery of my linguistic competence made a fool of me. However, I could understand very well that he was full of scorn for his own generation, who were relying on the students at Athens University to show the courage they lacked.

And what about England? England, I said, was full of strikes, economic crises and loud social confrontations. 'That sounds wonderful. Because listen –' Vassili indicated the street – 'What do you hear?'

I said, 'It sounds very quiet.'

'It *is* very quiet. Athens is very quiet! Aristophanes is banned and no one says anything! That is the one joke they have left us.'

Elektra was not on the island. We stayed a couple of weeks in the cottage, but things were changing in the Cyclades. Some Americans, who were terribly friendly, were building a house between us and the sea. They were bringing in electricity and, of course, running water. The next year we went to France. We promised ourselves we would go to Greece again after the Colonels fell, if they ever did. Our absences from London meant that I gave up my Greek lessons and lost contact with Loukas.

Then the Colonels did fall. I went to a rally to celebrate the recall of Constantine Karamanlis to Athens. In the crowd, I saw Loukas. He was balder and scrawnier and greyer and more myopic than ever. 'At last!' I said. 'This is a happy day.'

'It could have been happier.'

'When are you going back?'

'I may go to America,' Loukas said. 'There is a danger of a right-wing backlash, backed – of course – by the CIA. There are things that have to be said, even if they are not popular.'

'What about Elektra and the children? Will they go with you?'

He looked at me as if I had all but vanished over his horizon. 'I have told Elektra that she should not wait for me. I have told her that I have changed. One must be a man about certain things.'

'I don't know if I ought to say this, Loukas, but I happen to know that what you think happened never happened. Never. I would stake my life on it. You can trust Vassili absolutely.'

He puffed his lips slightly, as if it was hardly worth wasting further words trying to educate me. 'I *do* trust Vassili,' he said. He turned and was looking in the crowd. His attention and mine was caught by a woman in a red anorak, with unruly dyed blonde hair, who was addressing a Labour politician in a very caustic manner over his government's complicity with the fallen Colonels.

'She could go fifteen rounds with Mohammed Ali, that one.'

He said, 'Evgenia is the woman I intend to make my new life with.'

'*What?*'

'Are you shocked? You are shocked.'

I said, 'But . . . but how *can* you? Vassili . . . Elektra . . . they . . . he . . . she . . . And all this time . . .'

'There is no comparison.'

'Of course there's a bloody comparison.'

He put an arm round the brassy blonde in the anorak. 'Not at all,' he said. 'Evgenia is not the wife of my friend.'

'I don't understand.'

'You don't understand because you will never be a Greek. *Pote, pote, pote!* Never, never, never.'

PERFECT STRANGERS

Richard Burns

Richard Burns was born in Sheffield in 1958. He was a regular reviewer for *The Independent* and taught creative writing at Lancaster University. He published seven novels: *A Dance for the Moon*, (a prize winner in the Jonathan Cape/*Sunday Times* First Novel Competition), *The Panda Hunt*, *Why Diamond Had to Die*, *Fond and Foolish Lovers* (runner-up in the 1990 John Llewellyn Rhys Award), *Sandro and Simonetta*, and the two fantasies, *Khalindaine* and *Troubadour*. He died in 1992.

PERFECT STRANGERS was first broadcast on Radio 4, read by Michael Maloney.

PERFECT STRANGERS

While you levelled the caravan I explored the site. 'Don't be long,' you called.

'Okay, Dad.'

There was a clubhouse with a shop, a games room, and a bar that was closed at that time of day. It was less dark in the games room, where the light had a different quality. It was a basement. Sunlight blanched through high windows, bounced on the ping-pong table, and reclined in the angle between floor and walls. I lifted a sad, bald table tennis bat from the bench beneath the windows, weighed it in my hand, put it down. I flicked a handle of the table football machine: the goalkeeper somersaulted obligingly but I'd no shilling to release the ball. I picked a beerbottle from a crate of empties and let it drop, noisily, back into its slot. Flies harassed the lampshade. Water wriggled through exposed pipes. It was all the same to me. I found a ping-pong ball under the table but its shell had cracked at the seam.

I would have left, had others not arrived. There were three of them, two boys and a girl. One boy was thin and older than me, the other was my age and fatter. The girl was pretty and younger, and smiled. 'Hello,' they said. They spoke eagerly, as though bored with one another and seeking diversion.

'Hi.'

'You new?' asked the thin youth. He was tall and pale, suited to subterranean light. 'What do they call you?'

'I'm Stephen Treece,' I said.

'Pleased to meet you. I'm Larry Adenau.' He spelt the alien surname as he offered his slim hand. I received both with uncertainty. My experience did not include youths with strange names who shook hands. 'This is Charles,' Larry added, 'and this is my sister Rebecca.'

'What school you go to?' asked Charles. 'I'm starting at Lancing next term.'

I went to a school of neither glamour nor reputation, a state school in Sheffield, but Charles was only interested in making his statement and had no use for my reply. 'You playing table tennis?' he asked me. 'Larry doesn't play and I thrash Rebecca.'

'I'll play if you like,' I said. 'But I've no bat.'

'It's okay.' Charles unzipped a fat padded bat from its fat padded case. 'There are some down here. You can use one of them.'

'That's not fair,' said Rebecca. 'The bats here are useless. You lend Stephen yours.'

'Call me Steve,' I said.

Charles explained what was wrong with Rebecca's suggestion. 'My father says no one can borrow mine, and anyway it's got special weights in so he couldn't use it anyway.'

'Borrow Bec's,' said Larry. 'Run back to the caravan and get it,' he told her.

'You get it,' she said, but went anyway.

'She's all right really,' said Larry as she left. 'You got a brother or sister, Steve?'

'One of each. But they're both older than me: Paula's married and Robert's with his friends on a barge holiday.'

'Which school you say you went?' Larry asked.

'Just an ordinary school. A comprehensive.'

'Oh, tough luck. I'm a Salopian myself. Michael Palin was in my house. You like *Monty Python*? It's brilliant.'

'It's rubbish,' said Charles. 'What you think of it, Steve?'

I was young. I had not heard of Michael Palin or *Monty Python*. I did not know what a Salopian was. Rebecca came back. I had no opinions but at least now I had a bat. 'Let's play,' I said.

'I'll score,' said Rebecca.

We bounced the ball back and forth across the table. Charles was aggressive but clumsy. These days I sometimes drive past Lancing College. I cannot pass the squatting rump of its chapel without thinking of Charles and his crouchbacked stance at the table tennis table. He stood with his face down and his eyes staring up through his brows. 'Play for serve,' he said, and we did.

The ball pattered damply back and forth. The table was old but the surface was true. I knew I would win.

Rebecca called out the scores. Seven-one, seven-two, eight-two, change-of-serve, two-eight. By the second game I was talking to Larry and Rebecca during points. 'What's your father do?' Rebecca asked.

'He's a sort of lecturer. In a college.' I didn't know you well, Dad. I barely knew you at all. 'What's yours do?'

'Is he a professor, your father?' Rebecca continued.

'No.'

'Our dad's a professor.'

'Oh.'

Charles overhit a backhand and I fetched the ball. 'How old are you two?' I asked.

'I'm fifteen,' said Larry. 'Bec's twelve. And you?'

'Thirteen. I'm fourteen in October.'

'Five-fifteen, Steve to serve, fifteen-five,' Rebecca called.

I served. Charles missed. 'Let!' he called.

'Wasn't!' said Rebecca.

'Was so!' insisted Charles.

'I don't mind,' I said. I could afford to be generous. 'We'll play a let.'

'He's cheating,' said Rebecca.

'Shut up,' said Charles. I served again. 'You're putting me off,' he said as his return hit the ceiling.

'Sixteen-five.'

'And anyway I wasn't ready.'

'Oh, for goodness sake,' said Larry. 'You lost the point. Umpire's decision.'

'You're not the umpire,' Charles argued. 'Rebecca is.'

'It's my ball and I'm going home!' mocked Rebecca.

Charles wasn't easily shamed. 'That's right,' he said, and went.

Rebecca laughed tidily. 'Silly boy.'

'He's all right really,' said Larry. 'Got the hots for Rebecca, that's all.'

Her face screwed up in pantomine disgust as we followed Larry up the stairs and into the furious sunlight. The clubhouse, an elegant Regency villa, faced an unkept lawn; beyond was the North Sea and a liquid sky that bridged the wide horizons. A rabbit flopped onto the lawn. It was gooey-eyed and sniffling. 'Myxamatosis,' Larry commented. 'Poor bugger.' The lawn was thatched with marram grass, tough and spikey, and the soil in the baked borders was red. The rabbit staggered towards the cliff and disappeared into the undergrowth.

'Which way's your parents' caravan?' Rebecca asked.

'My dad's,' I corrected. I lived with mum, went on holiday with you. It seemed a normal arrangement to me then. 'That way,' I told them, pointing. 'In the trees.'

'Not by the pond, I hope,' Rebecca said. 'You'll be bitten to death.'

'It's true,' said Larry. 'Midges the size of racehorses. Our van's over there too, but by the clifftop.'

We walked to the edge of the cliff. The Adenau family caravan, a large permanent one, jutted purposefully through the trees. I looked out over the sea. It was the first time I had seen the sea that year, but I was too old, or too young, to be excited.

'You've not been here before,' announced Larry.

'No.' Between the shingle and the sea was a margin of sand colonised by a few bright windbreaks. Toddlers tested the waves.

'Thought not,' said Larry. 'That's Dunwich over there.' He pointed north. 'You heard about Dunwich? Used to be a big port, but it's mostly under the sea now, and then it was a Rotten Borough like Old Salem, with a Member of Parliament who had no one to represent. Can you see the church? That's Greyfriars.' I thought of Billy Bunter. 'Churchyard is falling into the sea. Every high tide a few more graves are washed out of the cliff side and a few more skeletons are swept away.' He laughed. I couldn't tell Greyfriars from the rest of the long low coast but I could picture high midnight seas plucking the coffins from the cliffs, overturning the tombstones, spilling cadavers into the eerie dark. Meanwhile another blind rabbit stumbled into sight and crickets thrummed in the sandwort. 'And in the other direction that's Minsmere, the bird reserve.'

'That's the reason we come here every year,' said Rebecca. 'Dad's a birdwatcher.'

'Mine's not,' I said. 'Are you a birdwatcher too?'

'Larry sometimes goes with him,' she said. 'Bor-or-oring.'

'Bores me as well.' I was beginning to get the hots for her too.

'You seen Sizewell?' asked Larry. 'The atomic power station. It's down the coast.'

I got a pang of guilt then, thinking about you. 'I suppose I ought to get back to my dad,' I said. 'He'll be wondering where I am.'

'Right,' said Larry. 'We'll see you around. This evening perhaps? At the games room? Or there's a TV lounge: *Doctor Who*'s on soon. We'll see you somewhere anyway.'

'I expect so,' I said, and went back to the caravan.

Tea was beans on toast. The beans had burnt in the pan and there was a fresh plaster on the back of your hand. I thought you would be annoyed because I had gone off; instead you seemed anxious to please, making me a shandy from your can of Long Life and asking what I'd been doing. 'I met some interesting people,' I said. 'Rebecca and Larry Adenau. Their father's a birdwatcher too, and he's a professor.'

'That's nice.' You never made it to professor, did you Dad. A quick heart attack the year before retirement was your reward from the college.

The caravan wasn't level, and my shandy sloped awkwardly against the rim of my glass.

After tea I had my only chore, which was to lug the resentful weight of the water-carrier back from the standpipe. I hated that water-carrier. I hated that standpipe. 'Do you want to go for a walk?' you asked when I got back.

I'd wanted to watch *Doctor Who* with Larry and Rebecca but it was too late for that now. 'Not really,' I admitted.

'Just along the beach. I've not seen the sea yet.'

'All right.'

27

We walked along the shoreline. Flies rose from seaweed, and the setting sun loitered behind pale cloud and lowered itself towards the sea. A beachful of pebbles is a lot less interesting than an individual stone. One stone has beauty but a lot of stones is a heap. But a lot of water is more interesting than a drop. We walked towards Minsmere. If we spoke I can't remember a word of it. We probably said nothing at all. Birds lifted from the marshes in wheeling chorus and settled again in new patterns. We went back to the clubhouse. You bought me a bottle of lemonade.

Larry and Rebecca weren't in the games room or the TV lounge, though Charles was in the latter. He smiled at me in a friendly way. It was growing darker outside. Moths worried the lightbulbs, and Charles's watch had luminous hands as well as many dials. It would, he told me, function at fifteen fathoms, and he used it to tell me the time in Tokyo and New York until I decided I should see what my dad was doing. You were doing badly, I guess, sitting on your own with a book and a pint. We went back to the caravan together, and boasted what pleasant times we'd each had.

The next day I saw the Adenaus again. They were not much alike. While he was all wrists, shins, ribs, she was busty even then, round-faced, brown-eyed, brown-haired and brown-skinned. 'Are you doing anything today?' asked Larry.

'Not really,' I said.

'Fancy coming to Walberswick with us.'

'Sure. I'll have to ask my dad though.'

'We'll come with you.'

On the way I explained that my parents were divorced. Divorce was unusual in those days, I suppose, and they looked at you with curiosity, but if they hoped to sees signs of notoriety or dissipation they were disappointed. So were you. 'I thought we might go out ourselves.'

'It's all right. I won't be long.'

We went back to the Adenaus' caravan, then drove off in the Professor's Merc. Walberswick was neat and unmemorable, but I walked around with Larry and Rebecca, had lunch outside a pub with their parents, and then went down to the sea. There was an eight-track player in the car and Mrs Adenau played Mozart as we drove through the delicate swelling of Suffolk. Rebecca let me hold her hand. In the evening I played ping-pong against Charles again, and this time it was for Rebecca's attention.

I fell a little in love with both Rebecca and Larry, in fact, and started going to their caravan first thing in the morning, staying there till tea. Professor and Mrs Adenau were rarely there. They were hunting avocet and phalaropes in the marshes of Minsmere, and in that caravan, at various times, Larry showed me his collection of grey Penguin Modern Classics. And Rebecca? To begin with she was stern. The scorecard was fairly simple: one point for kissing, two for French kissing, three for touching her bra, four for touching her breast, five for the fabled triumph, six for going all the way. Larry was reading on the grass outside; I had reached four, a personal best. But it seemed I would get no further.

'Please,' I pleaded.

'No,' she said.

I tried to kiss her into submission but had no expertise. We wrestled: it was undignified but it seemed she still liked me. 'You can't touch,' she conceded. 'But you can have a look if you like.'

My breathing was difficult.

So she showed me. I saw an unspectacular fold in the flesh guarded by twists of dark bald, and though I did not know how to score it according to the standard system the memory of that secret place kept me company for years.

Penguin Modern Classics became an equally treasured companion. I admired the quiet authority with which they stood on Larry's shelves, and bought *Goodbye to Berlin* by Christopher Isherwood in that edition, when I went with the Adenaus to Framlingham. I remember you nodding when I showed the purchase. 'I am a camera,' you quoted, 'my shutter open.' I took it to the games room that evening and, while Rebecca played Charles at table tennis and the younger children played table football, Larry and I sat in the inadequate light of some forty-watt bulbs and read grey-spined Penguins with bright abstract covers.

A fortnight went by and then it was time to leave. I had acquired *The Great Gatsby* by then. And, one rainy afternoon in Rebecca's caravan while the rain put a pattern on the thin tin roof, I had seen her completely naked, as she exchanged her bikini for something more suited to wet weather. 'No touching,' she warned again as, with the Venetian blinds drawn, she danced for me briefly in a pattern of smooth flanks. She leant over, still naked, and kissed me on the forehead while I gawped. Then we thought we heard Larry coming back, or maybe her parents, and by the time we had discovered it was a false alarm the moment had gone. I promised I would write. Rebecca wrote once, a rather chatty girlish letter from her boarding school. I could think of no reply. And then they had gone, like the moment, Larry and Rebecca, though I guess they retained some kind of power over me. I studied English literature and thought about sex a lot at university.

You took me straight home to Mum, the clumsy caravan still fastened to the back of your Maxi. 'I'll not come inside,' you said. 'Your mum might have visitors.'

This didn't seem likely but I wasn't going to argue. 'Thanks then,' I said.

'I'm glad you enjoyed it.'

'Oh Dad, I did. Really. The best holiday ever.'

And you drove off, as you always drove off, alone.

Which would be the end of the story, except for the postcard of the Minsmere cliffs pinned above your bedhead, the one I found when I cleared your effects. The colour had gone from the picture, except where the head of the pin had been, washing a once blue sky to a more credible grey. There was no stamp, nor was the card addressed. But there was a message, in bolder handwriting than you usually used. 'Stephen called it the best holiday he's had. I'm so proud, so happy!'

TAM O' SHANTER

Donna Tartt

Donna Tartt is the author of *The Secret History*. She has written stories for *The New Yorker* and *Harpers*, and currently lives in New York.

TAM O' SHANTER was published in *The New Yorker* and broadcast on Radio 4. It was read by Harry Towb.

TAM O' SHANTER

The Children's Hospital was cheery enough, thought Gordon
– as far as hospitals went. Still there was no way they could
get rid of that antiseptic smell, and the alien trappings of
childhood irritated him and made him uncomfortable. High
voices, pop music, bright murals of cartoon creatures that
he didn't recognise. Teapots with dotty faces? Ogling crabs
and tuna fish? Medical apparatus lined the chill, windowless
corridors, which echoed like the corridors of a ship in deep
space. A young nurse, young enough to be his granddaughter –
maybe she was a doctor, with the trousers and the stethoscope;
he had never got used to lady doctors – walked humming past
him, a bouquet of lollipops blooming from the breast pocket of
her white coat.

The first film he'd ever been in, half a century before – *Our
Mutual Friend*, Joan Fontaine, Larry Olivier, 1936 – there had
been a scene in a children's hospital. Gordon was seven years
old, an extra, lying in an iron bed on a set in Twickenham with
black circles painted under his eyes. He and Dolores had stayed
up late to watch it on television about six months ago. Sitting
there in the curtained sunroom with his decaf coffee and his
low-salt popcorn, and seeing the little face – plump and healthy
even under the make-up – which had somehow, unbelievably,
once been his own, all he could remember was how he had
stealthily attempted to flatten a wad of chewing gum against
the roof of his mouth as the arc lights blazed red through his
closed eyelids. Later, between takes, he'd watched some of
the older kids pretend to get drunk off the dregs of a bottle
of Scotch that they said they'd stolen from Miss Fontaine but
had actually come from the make-up man. He and a girl his own

age, annoyed at being excluded, had turned their attention to pinching a smaller boy until he cried. It was to be the most prestigious film Gordon would appear in in his entire career, though he would not become aware of this for another twenty years or so. And it *was* a fine film. It stood up, even now. Alec Guinness had done an excellent job as the old Jew.

The garish cartoon faces on the wall – green-armoured space creatures, with slitted bandit kerchiefs tied around their eyes – goggled down at him: with a sinking feeling, he became aware of the first, timorous lurch of the now familiar nausea. Fried eggs didn't sit so well with the roentgens. They had tasted good in the coffee shop but he'd known he'd be sorry later.

He'd been in the States for fifty years, had almost lost his accent, though even when he was a kid it had all been largely phoney, all those Geordie MacTavish phrases like 'wee braw lassie' and 'och the noo'. His real name was Gordon Burns, but in the pictures he'd been Geordie MacTavish for six years. Geordie MacTavish the Highland Lad: Geordie rescuing hurt animals, Geordie breaking up smugglers' rings and fighting the Nazis, Geordie sent away to public school. Twelve years old and skipping around in a bloody kilt like Bonnie Prince Charlie, sneaking smokes between the takes with the cameramen. Then the contract with Paramount, bit parts in costume dramas. He hadn't been in a film in thirty-five years. For the past thirty, he'd lived in Burbank with Dolores, in the same little pink stucco bungalow they'd bought when they were newlyweds, working on his golf game and doing public relations for one of the big production companies. He'd never been all that fond of PR. But since he'd had to retire, he'd missed it desperately. Away from the camaraderie of the shared routine, the office acquaintances had begun to slip. And he didn't see too many other people on a regular basis, not even in the neighbourhood where he had lived for so long.

He was definitely feeling ill now. He wished Dolores were with him. He wanted to turn around and go back home. But how could you refuse a request like this? His doctor had told him about the little girl. Down at the Cancer Center in San Diego, he'd said, a bit of a drive, but it would mean so much; old stills of Gordon all over the walls and even a Dandie Dinmont terrier – named, of course, Bobbie, after Gordon's sidekick in the series. Nine years old and dying of leukaemia – some chromosomal kind, nearly always fatal. 'She watches your movies before she goes into chemo,' the doctor had said. 'Says Geordie's never afraid and neither is she.' What a rotten world, thought Gordon.

He wouldn't mind it so much if he stood any chance of actually cheering the poor kid up. But no matter how their parents tried to prepare them, warned them again and again that the films had been made fifty years before, children were always disappointed not to see another child. Sometimes the younger ones didn't understand. They asked him where the real Geordie was. Was he Geordie's grandpa? But the older ones could scarcely conceal their dismay. He would never forget the afternoon several years before when a little girl – grandchild of a colleague at the production company – had been brought to meet him. Gamely, he had pulled out the hat, the old red tam o' shanter. Gamely, he had answered the door, bending low to greet the little girl and booming: 'Aye, then! And who's this wee lassie?' He would never forget the look on the little girl's face. It was a look of shocked recognition, then of dawning horror: as if it were her own death she saw, leaning down so close to greet her. As if she could see the ruin of the boy he had been – destroyed now, lost for ever – buried deep beneath his sagging cheeks.

They kept the air-conditioners in these places turned up far too high. It was August outside, summer blazing away, though you'd never know it here. A towering man in a satin tracksuit, with freakishly elongated limbs and the placid face of a camel walked past. (Basketball player? thought Gordon.) He was carrying a tiny, too silent child. 'So how you and your dad like to come watch the guys practise, Slice?' he was saying. Huge-eyed and staring, the child clung to his long neck like a baby monkey, tracking Gordon with its gaze, as it was borne

35

down the gleaming hall. Even the bandages on its tiny wrists and ankles were covered with cartoons.

For a moment, he felt a queer sharp pang of what was almost jealousy. These kids were just too little. They didn't understand what it was all about. They didn't know what it was to be really afraid. He hadn't lived like a lot of those fellows in the business; those guys deserved what they got. But he'd lived a quiet life and a sober one – one cocktail before dinner, regular exercise, early to bed. Gave up the cigarettes at thirty-three, before they even knew how bad the damned things were. Last year, at sixty-two, they'd finally caught up. The crowning inequity in a life full of bad deals. He'd joked sourly with Dolores, after they'd put him on the stuff that made him lose his dinner, that at least he was already bald, at least he wasn't going to lose his hair.

He paused outside the door. It stood partly open, waiting for his arrival. He fumbled in his coat pocket for the tam and – glancing at the ghost of his reflection in the chill glass of a reception area opposite – placed it at a jaunty, Geordie-like angle on his bald head. The dim outline of his face shocked him. Dentures; flaccid cheeks; pouches under the eyes. His nose was as pinched as a dead man's. 'Maybe it'll be a comfort to the poor kid after all,' he thought. 'To see what she'd have to look forward to, to die and know what she's not missing'.

He nudged the door open. Instantly a couple of anxious parents – young, kids themselves, really – rose nervous and smiling from their bedside chairs. But his fleeting impression of them was broken by a welcoming bark, a small grey blur dashing recklessly to meet him: 'Bobbie,' he thought, 'Bobbie.' And he was knocked nearly breathless by a mysterious surge of joy. He glanced up. Everywhere he looked, his own lost face stared back at him, from rain-swept piers and rocky landscapes, from the thundery dark of the artificial skies: magical, defiant, impossibly young. Then, with a jolt, he became aware of the little girl. She was sitting up in bed, propped on pillows and looking at him attentively. Tiny hands, like bird claws, rested on the edge of the coverlet. Her face was mottled with broken capillaries. She was as ugly and as fragile as a new-hatched chick. But there was a composure, a sweet intelligence about the eyes that regarded him calmly from the grotesque little face. On her head, as bald as his own, was perched a little red tam o' shanter.

Suddenly he was struck hard, by a shudder of nausea: barking dog, chorus of photographs, the stare of his own heartless young eyes. The little girl – cruel plastic butterfly, which hid the needle of her IV, perched bright on the tender veins of her wrist – was looking at him with a good-humoured, impartial welcome, as if he were a stranger whose eyes she had chanced to meet while scanning for the face of a long-awaited loved one. And then she smiled, as though he were the best thing she'd ever seen, as though she'd been waiting for him all her life. 'Hello, Geordie,' she said.

The little dog was mad with excitement. It spun around him, barking in circles as he went across the room to her, his arms held out to her tiny, bruised arms, which she stretched out to greet him, the wings of the stinging blue butterfly brushing his cheeks. Lover to lover. Ruin to ruin. 'Hello,' he said to her, bending low, in a voice so boyish it surprised him. 'Hello, me wee Highland lassie.'

SUSPICION

Deborah Moggach

Deborah Moggach has written ten novels, a stage play and a book of short stories. She has adapted her novel, *The Stand In*, as a Hollywood screenplay, and is adapting her latest novel, *The Ex-Wives*, as a television serial. She lives in London with her two teenage children.

SUSPICION was first broadcast on Radio 4, read by Barbara Flynn.

SUSPICION

He seemed such a normal bloke. That's how they get away with it I suppose, looking normal. He looked like a real football-playing, I'm-in-sales, make-mine-a-double-scotch sort of bloke. That's what attracted me in the first place. After the waifs and strays I'd been out with he seemed so male. I mean, he actually looked as if he could drive a car.

His name was Kenneth McTurk and I met him when he came in for a glass of guava juice. He'd just been to the acupuncturist upstairs – the café where I work, it's in this building full of ists, reflexologists, aromatherapists, all that alternative stuff that's not so alternative any more since Prince Charles took it up.

He sat at the counter, rubbing his back. 'By Jesus, I feel like a pin-cushion,' he said. 'You seen the size of those needles?'

He had an Irish accent – beguiling, almost female in such a beefy man. He had a ruddy face and sticking-out ears; they gave him a boyish look. He wore a suit – *nobody* wore a suit in our place. He was one of those fidgety men who are always jangling their car keys. He said that he was a martyr to his back, stress-related said his doctor, and why not give acupuncture a whirl? So he had looked it up in the Yellow Pages.

'A load of mumbo-jumbo, my love, if you're asking my opinion,' he said. 'Now would you recommend the carrot cake?' I said it was made with bran. 'I see I've entered a bowel-friendly environment,' he replied. 'I suppose a cheroot is out of the question?'

It was, but the place was empty. So he had a smoke and we introduced ourselves.

'Velda,' he said. 'Now that's unusual.'

'It means wise woman.' I laughed. When it came to men, never had anybody been so ludicrously mis-named.

*

The next day, when I was cashing up, he walked in and said he was taking me out for a drink. Well, why not? He made me feel flushed and reckless. As we walked towards his car he stopped at the Natwest, plucked a sprig of fuchsia from its windowbox, and put it into my hair. When we arrived at his car he blithely removed a *Doctor on Emergency Call* sticker from the windscreen.

'I know you're not a doctor,' I said. 'What *do* you do?'

'Bit of this, bit of that.' He tapped the side of his nose with his finger. 'Import export.'

Until then I had only seen dodgy men on TV series. I suppose I lived a sheltered existence, me and my cats and the long-running non-event of my love-life. Suddenly here I was, sitting in a flash car with an unknown middle-aged man who jumped the lights and filled the air with cheroot smoke. He said the acupuncturist had been a con-artist and I said boldly: 'Takes one to know one.'

He laughed and told me about a practical joke he had played on somebody, a bloke he'd once worked with. He had filled the drawers of the chap's desk with water and put a lot of goldfish in them. Did I believe him? Who cares. It was so insanely silly that I fell in love with him, then and there.

He took me to a pub in Kilburn. It was big and noisy. Two fiddlers played, they were called the McDougal Brothers, and I drank a pint of Guinness – me, Velda, who was usually in bed by ten with a cup of herbal tea. There was a raffle for a fluffy elephant and I didn't want to join in because it was so hideous but Kenneth insisted. 'Fund-raising,' he said.

'Funds for what?'

But he just put his finger on the side of his nose. I hadn't a clue what he was talking about but by then everything was getting swimmy and suddenly there was this furry thing in my arms – not Kenny but the elephant, I had won it – and I was in his car and next thing we were sitting in a restaurant drinking champagne and the next thing I remember it was Kenneth in my arms and my duvet over us and the sound of my cats scratching at the kitchen door where I had shut them away.

*

A couple of weeks later he moved in. Not that he brought much with him – just a suitcase of clothes. But there he was, a full-grown man, knocking into the furniture and whistling in my bathroom – he even managed to whistle while he shaved, 'My Way' with a buzzing accompaniment. I bought him Ty-Phoo teabags and – proof of my love – bacon for breakfast. I'm a vegetarian, you see, and the smell drives me wild. With him in it, six-foot-two, my flat looked stuffy and spinsterly, with its batik hangings and its bowls of pot-pourri, but he said it was so peaceful. He said it was like stepping into another world, a bedouin tent with just me and him.

'It's a battlefield out there, Velda my love,' he said, lying on the bed with his arms around the elephant. A joss-stick spiralled smoke one side and a cheroot spiralled smoke on the other. 'You've no idea of it.'

He charmed me. He even charmed Mrs Prichard upstairs, carrying her shopping and flirting with her, though she's eighty-three. He made me feel as if I was the most bewitching woman in the world, my skin blushed, I bloomed for him. He told me I was beautiful, voluptuous, a goddess. He wrote lewd suggestions in the steam on the bathroom mirror. And flowers, oh the flowers! When he arrived late, the nodding heads of them wrapped in fancy paper from the all-night shop in Westbourne Grove.

He often arrived late and left early. Or he would be home for the afternoon and leave after supper. He never got any phone calls and I never met any of his friends but I didn't mind, he and I were cocooned in ourselves, we had no need of anything. My job at the café was part-time so I fitted in with him. As for his job – well, he was very mysterious about it. He only said it involved a lot of travel and in fact he was away a great deal, days on end sometimes. I wasn't suspicious. Believe it or not, I wasn't even suspicious when I found the handcuffs. Or not for the right reason.

It happened like this. Kenny had been living with me for two weeks and we had just come home from the pictures. I realised I had left my shawl in his car so I found his jacket, which was hanging up in the hallway, and fished for his car keys. In the pocket I felt something heavy, wrapped in a paper bag. I took it out. Just at that moment he came out of the kitchen. I held out the pair of handcuffs and laughed.

'Oh oh, bondage-time!'

His face reddened. Then he recovered himself and laughed. 'Tie me up!' He shoved a cloth in my hand. 'Here, the killer tea towel! Whip me to a frenzy! I like it, I like it!'

Another odd thing happened that evening. He said he was just popping out for some cheroots. I watched him from the window. Why? I don't know. He crossed the street and walked towards Westbourne Grove. But he stopped at the phone box on the corner, looked around, and went in. I watched him – a small, solitary figure in the illuminated booth. Somebody familiar always shrinks, don't they, when they think they are unobserved. Why was he making a secret phone call? In my area of Bayswater the phone booths are plastered with hookers' cards – *I'm Lorraine, Spank Me! Strict French Lessons!* I remember thinking: suppose he *is* a bondage-freak. That's why he's always popping out. He's ringing up one of them now. Lorraine or someone.

I didn't say anything. He was away too much for me to spoil our short times together by wife-type accusations. The next morning, however, he seemed edgy and abstracted. When I went into the bedroom, after breakfast, he was shoving a pair of muddy trainers into a carrier bag. When he saw me he stopped, dropped the bag behind the bed and put his arms around me.

'I have to go away for a couple of days,' he said. 'Oh Velda my lovely, if you knew how much I wished it was you and me alone in the world, far away from all this.'

'From all what?'

'It's dangerous out there, see. A man, he's weak. Maybe he's young and foolish. He makes a mistake maybe once in his life and then he's caught like a fly in a spider's web. They have him there, where they want him. He can run, but he can't hide. He can hide, but he can't run.'

He kissed the tip of my nose and then he was gone, carrier bag and all.

That night there was an explosion in the Territorial Army Barracks in Albany Street, near Regent's Park. Four men were injured – it was a miracle it wasn't more – but half the place was gutted. The IRA claimed responsibility and issued a statement saying it was stepping up its mainland terrorist campaign.

I don't read the newspapers. I'm not a political sort of person. I saw it by chance on the front page of a *Guardian* that somebody had left in the café. Nothing clicked together, not even then. Nothing clicked until the following Thursday.

Kenneth had been back for a couple of days. Was it my imagination or was he changing? He looked fleshier – he was putting on weight. Maybe it was my lentil lasagne. And he snapped at Flapjack, my Burmese, when she was only playing with his shoelaces.

It was early evening and I had to nip out to the shops. Halfway down the street, however, I realised I had forgotten my purse so I went back and let myself into the flat. Kenny was in the bedroom, speaking on the phone. I paused in the hallway.

'Let me speak to Fergus,' he said in a low voice. There was a pause, then he said: 'Fergus, you keep away from that gun, see? You put it down or I'll be telling Mr Connolly. And you wouldn't like that, would you?'

I let myself out of the flat and crept downstairs. I managed to make it to the end of the street and leaned against some railings. My heart hammered against my ribs. How could I have been so stupid? The shock was so great that when I tried to pull the facts together I had to haul them, slowly, as if I were drugged.

The handcuffs. The Republican pub in Kilburn. The terrorist explosion . . . The long, unexplained absences . . . The phone box and now the threatening telephone call . . .

Funnily enough I wasn't alarmed, not for myself. In fact I felt a shameful tingle of excitement. This man I loved was suddenly strange to me. It didn't cross my mind, not yet, that he might be dangerous – that he might, in fact, be a killer. The whole thing seemed as disconnected and unlikely as some TV drama I happened to have stepped into, the sort of TV drama I never watched anyway, that was happening to someone else.

I was in the late-night supermarket, standing in front of a pork chop. A kidney nestled in the pallid flesh. I thought: I came out to buy some dinner and now a different Kenneth will be eating it. To someone like me a meat counter smells of death; it lurks there, inert, under the cellophane. I knew I mustn't think like this – I mustn't even *start* to think about killing or I wouldn't be able to behave normally when I got home. What was I supposed to be buying anyway? My mind was a blank. Beside me a Rastafarian dipped up and down to the beat of his walkman; a woman shouldered me aside and pulled out a pack of sausages. Trolleys rattled and a tannoy boomed but it came from a thousand miles away. I had to get through this evening somehow, walk it through like a robot, until tomorrow came, Kenneth left for work and I could start to think clearly.

I went back home and let myself into the flat.

'Light of my life!' He pounced at me from behind and pinioned me against the wall. 'Five minutes you've gone, and it's an eternity!' His breath was hot on my face.

It had been an eternity. I had stepped out of one life and into another. Nothing would be the same, ever again.

It rained in the night. The next morning dawned shiny and innocent, the streets washed clean. I kissed Kenneth goodbye. The puddles winked at me. In the block of flats opposite someone opened a window, flashing a message to me. Or to him? Where was he going?

'Where are you going?' I asked.

'Liverpool,' he said, quick as anything. 'A shipment's coming in.'

From Ireland? I couldn't bear to ask him. By questioning him, I felt it was me who was doing the betraying, not him. Ridiculous, I know.

His hair was slicked back, dark and wet, from the shower. His signet ring caught the sun as he scratched the side of his nose. I put my arms around him and held him tightly; silently I said goodbye to the old Kenneth. I smelt his familiar scent of tobacco and Eau Sauvage.

'There there,' he murmured, 'I'll be seeing you tomorrow.' He disentangled himself, glanced up and down the road and loaded his suitcase into the boot. I tried to help him but he wouldn't let me and slammed the boot shut. He was slightly breathless.

He drove off and I went inside, slowly. I felt very old. Mrs Prichard, hurrying downstairs, looked by comparison as spry as a girl.

'Is he gone, that naughty boy?' she asked, waving the *Daily Express*. 'I was going to tell him his stars.'

That's the only bit *I* used to read, I wanted to reply. The horoscopes. Now I understand why I never looked at the other pages.

'He likes to know it before he flies,' she said. 'These airline pilots are very superstitious.'

Oh Lord, he had lied to her, too.

I closed my front door. My cats pressed themselves against my legs. They pressed against his legs too, they didn't know the difference. I tried to practise my postural meditation but for once I couldn't concentrate. Squatting on the carpet, I stared at myself in the mirror: cloudy black hair, square face. Velda Mathews, aged thirty-one. All these years I had gone to groups and cultivated my inner space, hoping to find something there. Buddhism, I had tried. Psychotherapy, oh years of that. I had sat on beanbags, sobbing on strangers' shoulders and saying I loved them, but in truth it had been one big void. Then along came Kenneth, and suddenly I had come alive. Ironic, wasn't it? A man who spent his time blowing people to smithereens.

I switched on the radio. It was tuned, as usual, to Radio 3, but I fiddled around until I found some news.

'. . . a security alert in Central London . . . a soldier was shot dead in North Belfast . . .'

I switched it off, went into the bedroom and opened the wardrobe. His clothes hung there but I couldn't touch them. I didn't want to find anything out. I went to work in a daze and served a customer with gooseberry fool instead of guacamole. Margie, who ran the café, asked if anything was the matter but I didn't tell her because once I put it into words it would become real. Not only would I have to cope with her reaction – she adored crises – but I would have to decide what to do. Kick him out? Tell the police? Betray him, just as he had betrayed me? But maybe he had been protecting me, by his lies. You see, I didn't know how to react. My group told me how to cope with denial and rage and absence of self-worth but nobody told me how to cope with a possible murderer. We weren't used to that sort of thing. Parental damage was as far as we got.

He came home the next evening. He looked exhausted. We went to bed and he fell asleep, his leg a dead weight on mine. *It's dangerous, out there.* Down in the street, a police car wailed. *A man, he makes a mistake maybe once in his life and then he's caught.* Maybe he had joined when he was young and foolish, and now he could never escape. He was theirs for life, caught in a spiral of violence.

He turned over, grunting.

'If you're ever in trouble . . .' I murmured.

He sat up. 'And what trouble might that be?'

Down in the street a woman screeched with laughter. A car door slammed. I remembered my suspicions – when was it, only a week ago? Whipping a call-girl seemed such an innocent activity now. Noddyland compared to this. If only I could roll back time; if only we could start again from *there*.

He went back to sleep. It was unnerving, this body next to mine. The nearest sensation was when my friend Pauline had told me she was a lesbian. The pole-axing shock . . . the slow, skin-prickling realisation . . . the way I had to get to know this new Pauline all over again . . .

Suddenly I sat up. Yesterday morning, what had he been hiding from me, in the boot of his car?

I slid out of bed, wrapped myself in my kimono and crept into the hallway. I fished in his jacket pocket. How sharp and cold his keys felt, how solidly knobbly the St Christoper! Actually doing something, rather than harbouring vague suspicions, is shockingly physical. I went outside. It was freezing.

I unlocked the boot and opened it. Inside, half-hidden by a blanket, was a long, bulky-looking bag. Like a bag for golf clubs, that long. Only I knew there weren't golf clubs inside.

'Can I help you?'

I swung round. A police car had drawn up beside me; I heard the crackling static of a radio.

'Just . . . forgot something in the car,' I stuttered, and slammed the boot shut.

The next morning, at seven-thirty, the phone rang. I picked it up.
'Hello?'
There was no answer, just the sound of breathing. Down the line, faintly, I heard the sound of machine-gun fire. A muffled rat-a-tat-tat. Then the receiver was replaced.
Kenneth was sitting up in bed. 'Who was that?' he asked, sharply.
'Wrong number.'
Frying his bacon, half an hour later, I tried to be light-hearted.
'I don't know anything about you'.
'And what sort of thing might you be wanting to know, my petal?' His voice was light, too. I felt we were caught in some conspiracy together.
'Anything.' I slid the eggs onto his plate. 'I don't even know your hobbies.'
'Oh, I like to pull the wings off little girls.'
I tried to laugh. 'Well, sports then. What do you play. Tennis, golf?'
He paused. 'Golf, I enjoy. Trouble is, the people you meet.'
What did he mean – British imperialists or something? Anti-Republicans? 'Do you have a club?'
'Oh no, I play with my bare hands.'
'I mean, do you belong to a club?'
He tipped the ketchup bottle; red sauce slopped onto his plate. 'The Mountview. Why, my sweetheart?'

When he had gone I looked up the Mountview Club in the Yellow Pages. It was out in Enfield. I dialled the number.
'Er, I want to leave a message for one of your members,' I said. 'A Mr Kenneth McTurk.'
There was a shuffle of paper at the other end. Somebody was obviously looking at a list. Finally the voice said: 'We have no member of that name.'

*

That morning explosives were found in a Ford Transit van, parked in Chancery Lane. I read about it in the *Standard*; I read the papers every day now. *Please be vigilant*, said the Head of the Anti-Terrorist Squad. *You, the public, are our eyes and ears.* There had been a spate of kidnappings in Derry, too; the latest had been a local supermarket manager and his wife. Shamefully, I didn't consider the victims in all this or the political rights and wrongs. Love makes us myopically self-absorbed. I just thought: does he really care for me, or is he using me for my flat, a place where he can lie low?

When I got home that evening he was already there; his car was parked outside in the dark street. I let myself into the flat like a thief, like somebody who didn't belong there – criminality is catching. I paused outside my bedroom door. He was talking on the phone.

'What do you mean, *now*? I can't come now!' His voice was shrill; almost unrecognisable. 'Pipe down will you! Get a hold on yourself! They'll hear what you're saying!'

I went into the kitchen and stared at the piled-up sink. Ludicrously, I thought: can't even terrorists help with the washing-up? My eyes filled with tears.

'Forgive me, my lovely.'

I jumped. He was standing in the doorway. He looked terrible. His eyes were bloodshot and his tie was loose, like a drunkard's.

'I have to go out, see.'

'Why do you have to go out?' My voice rose. 'Why can't you tell me? Don't you trust me? Do you think I wouldn't understand?'

'I have no doubt whatsover, my darling, that you wouldn't understand. Nobody in their sane mind would understand.'

He kissed me and then he left, slamming the door behind him.

I ran downstairs. His car was pulling away from the kerb, its headlight beams weeping in the rain.

At that moment I took a decision, a split-second decision; a cab was passing and I stepped into the street.

'Follow that car!' I said.

The stagey words made the whole thing unreal. I was sucked into the momentum of a thriller. I clutched my handbag to my chest, swaying as we rounded corners, jolting as we shuddered to a stop at intersections. At one point we nearly lost Kenneth, but one of his tail-lights was broken so I could spot him ahead. To calm myself I chanted 'Om, om' but it suddenly seemed silly. Had I shut the front door? Would the cats get out? Had I got enough money for the fare, wherever we were going? The driver said nothing. I watched the sturdy back of his neck; beyond it the slewing wipers and the wobbling blobs of red. They smeared, rhythmically, across the windscreen.

Half an hour passed, maybe more. Then the cab stopped. We were somewhere in the suburbs. Large, Tudor-style houses loomed up on either side. Was this IRA headquarters? I fumbled for the fare; the driver didn't seem the slightest bit curious. Ahead of us Kenneth's car had stopped; its tail-lights were extinguished. I saw him climb out, open the boot and pull out the long, heavy bag. He paused, in the rain, looked up at one of the houses and walked slowly towards its front door.

I got out of the cab. The driver drove off. A woman hurried past me, her head down. I stopped her.

'Excuse me!' I hissed. 'Who lives there?'

'There?' She looked at the house. 'An estate agent.'

'Estate agent?'

'And his family.' She hurried off. I stood there, sodden.

It's odd, how one reacts in a situation like this. One can't tell beforehand, simply because it never arises. I felt disembodied, floating. Adrenalin fuelled me, like some emergency engine humming into life. I understood what was happening. He was going to kill this estate agent. Or take him hostage.

I ran towards the house. Kenneth had gone in. I rushed round the back, pushing through some wet bushes. From the ground floor came the sounds of gunfire – rat-a-tat-a-tat, machine-gun fire. I tried the kitchen door. It was open. I went in.

Upstairs I heard him shouting, and a woman's voice. 'You bastard!' she cried, over and over. 'You bastard!'

Downstairs the gunfire had stopped. I ran upstairs, two at a time. Light blazed on the landing. I heard their voices through a closed door. I flung it open.

He was standing in the bedroom with a woman. They swung round and stared at me.

'Velda!' he gasped.

'That's *her?*' said the woman. 'What's she doing here?'

My knees turned to water. I sat down, heavily, in a chair. Two boys came into the room; one of them carried a gun.

'Fergus! Dominic!' he said. 'Go back to the lounge, this minute!'

The boys looked at me, their eyes wide, and went out. Clatter-clatter went the gun against the banisters as they trailed downstairs.

The woman sat down on the bed. She was bleached blonde, and very good-looking. 'So that's her,' she said. 'She's a big girl, isn't she?'

There was a silence. Downstairs the TV came on. Kenneth, his face red, fumbled for a cheroot.

'Don't smoke that in here,' she said, 'you know I hate it.' He put the packet back in his pocket. He literally hung his head, like a small boy up in front of a headmistress. She was looking at me with dispassionate interest. 'I didn't know anyone wore kaftans any more.'

'Sally – '

He started to speak but she took no notice. She turned to me. 'You can have him. Do you know, Valerie or whatever it is – '

'Velda.'

'– I've actually been whistling around the house?' She flung herself back on the bed. 'Take him!' She gazed up at the chandelier. 'No more hoovering every day and keeping this huge bloody house nice, not that he'd notice, except he notices when it's not done, *and* trying to run my shop, not that I've had any support in *that* department . . .' Her voice grew dreamy. 'No more having to stop the boys fighting because it might disturb him, and clearing up their stuff but he says they should do it but if they did it it would never get done and then he'd get even more irritable, mmmm and letting them watch their ghastly videos . . .'

'I am *here*, you know,' he said.

'And he's getting so *fat*!' she said. 'It must be all those dinners he's eaten twice. First sitting chez moi and second sitting wherever you live.' She raised her head and looked at me. 'You obviously like your food too.'

'There's no need to talk to her like that!' he snapped.

She turned to him. 'I smelt a rat with that sudden interest in golf. You're such a lazy slob. Amazing I didn't guess. Tournaments in St Andrews, weekend championships God knows where. Coming back all muddy and shagged out. In a manner of speaking.' She started to laugh.

I turned to Kenneth. 'I didn't realise they were toy ones. The handcuffs.' I couldn't think of anything else to say.

'Take him!' cried Sally, tears of laughter streaming down her face. 'Take him! Make up your mind!'

I looked at Kenneth, and made up my mind.

I'LL SWING YOU
ROUND BY THE TAIL!

Julia O' Faolain

Julia O' Faolain is the author of *No Country for Young Men*, *The Irish Signorina* and most recently, *The Judas Cloth*. Married to the historian Lauro Martines, she divides her time between London and the continent. She is working on a collection of short stories.

I'LL SWING YOU ROUND BY THE TAIL was first broadcast on Radio 4, read by Sorcha Cusack.

I'LL SWING YOU
ROUND BY THE TAIL!

'Kick up tables kick up chairs, Kick old Jellybags down the stairs!'

The air fizzed with chalk from the dense, thick dusters which pupils were leaning out to beat on the classroom windowsills, but Miss Jill Bagley let their rowdiness pass. She looked as if she could already smell the soft air in the West where she'd be spending her summer holidays. Half there in spirit, her vowels had flattened and her eye had the vacant, country look of someone used to staring over empty, mesmeric space.

Maureen wasn't thinking of holidays. More importantly, this was her last day here: the end of school. THE END. In her head the word dilated as it did on cinema screens. She was fourteen and planned never to put foot in this dump again. The chalk dust mingled with a cloud of midges, making them whirr in panic.

Miss Bagley said something but Maureen didn't listen. Miss B. was an old maid who'd missed the boat.

'No more Latin,' yelled the kids behind her who were stacking benches, 'no more French! No more sitting on a hard old bench!'

The school didn't teach Latin or French. Only the three Rs. The rhyme had come from somewhere else. Maureen was planning to cut her hair and, if she could get the money, perm it in a golden frizz. She wanted to remake herself. Burst like a butterfly from her old, shrivelled self. It wouldn't be easy. With her father the way he was and Meg the way she was; Mammy said she'd need all Maureen's wages.

'Aw!' Maureen had complained.

'Blame your sister,' said Mammy. 'Blame Meg!'

Meg was in the family way and Mammy didn't think she could pass this baby off as her own. She was getting too old for the thing to be credible. Little Joe was three. He must be Meg's too. Meg worked hard. You had to hand her that. But if she had any more babies Maureen would never be able to keep her own money or make something of herself.

The priest, announced Miss Bagley, was here to say a few words to the senior class as it prepared to confront the challenges of adult life. Smiling, congratulatory, Father Creedon blessed and warned them in familiar phrases. His black waistcoat folded in readymade ripples like a concertina. Luckily, he sighed, the war would keep all but a few boys who planned to join the forces from leaving for the perils of pagan England. We must pray for those who did go that their faith would stand to them and be a comfort. And even those who stayed at home here in Ireland would need to remember the values which . . . Maureen thought of leaving now. Just walking out the door. Who could stop her? The light flowing in was the colour of shandy and the air was speckled with seeds and insects and tiny propellers from the sycamore tree outside. Her mind frothed. Scraps of songs drifted through it. Promises. 'There'll be bluebirds over/ The white cliffs of Dover/ Tomorrow, just you wait and see!' She'd heard that on the wireless. The priest mumbled exultantly, calling them all his dear children. She thought, I'll slip away! I'll be gone before they notice. In the end, though, she stayed to join in singing 'Faith of Our Fathers' and 'Auld Lang Syne'. There would be heaps of free days from now on.

She had a job waiting that Mammy said paid money for jam. Mammy washed clothes for a Mrs Connors who needed some-one to look after her kid.

'Just light work,' said Mammy whose arms were puffy from being in suds. She had muscles, but the flesh bubbled softly over them so that she looked sudsy even when she wasn't. There were few mangles in the houses where she worked and she'd got her muscles from wringing out sheets.

The Connors kid was a bit spoiled, but Maureen mustn't

slap her or do anything rough. She was to take her for walks so as to leave Mrs Connors free to write a book. Maureen had gone round to meet the pair of them when her Mammy was doing their laundry and the place smelled of boiled soap. There was a rose-garden and the soapy water was saved to spray the bushes. The kid's name was Jane. Aged seven. 'Very old-fashioned,' mumbled Mammy through a mouthful of clothes pegs. 'Talksh like she'sh shitting on the dictionary! Doesn't go to school. Her mother thinksh she'sh delicate.'

Maureen and Mammy had had their dinner in the kitchen while the family ate in what they called the 'dining-room'. They called 'dinner' 'lunch'. A maid called Bridie kept going back and forth.

'We get the same food as them.' Mammy put half a chicken into a bag she'd brought for the purpose. It was for Meg. 'Now you be nice to that child. No teasing her. She's not used to it. Just think of the wages you'll be earning. You can keep some for yourself,' Mammy decided, changing her mind. 'We'll manage. If your Dad would do a bit of digging we'd manage better, but there's no use praying for miracles.'

Dad's name was Joe which was why Little Joe would be called Little even if he grew to be six feet – if Dad lasted that long. Pickled in drink, he probably would. The smell of a cork set him off and he was in a constant daze.

'Push him away if he tries anything,' Mammy always warned. 'Then shout.' It was only recently that Maureen guessed what she meant.

Dawdling home, she was hailed by some older fellows who were working in a field tossing hay.

'Want to jump in it?' yelled Timmy Kelly, putting down his fork. 'Now's your chance before we tie down the cocks.' He had a lazy smile and his trousers were held up with a bit of string.

She was leery. Boys like that used double meanings and last year when she'd shouted that they should wash their mouths out with soap, some of them had rolled her in a ditchful of nettles. This lot seemed friendly enough, but she was too old for jumping in hay.

'Finished school then?' Timmy Kelly leaned on his fork. 'There's to be a hop later on above in the shelter. I'll be playing the accordion.'

She said she might come.

'I'll look out for you.' He was whistling 'You Are My Sunshine' as she moved off. One of his mates gave a wolf whistle and Maureen, feeling her adult life begin, tried to walk the way older girls did, swaying her hips a little and taking small steps. She wished she had high-heels.

' . . . my Double Woodbine,' faintly came Timmy Kelly's voice. 'You make me happy when skies are grey . . .'

The shelter was made of green corrugated iron and and was on the top of a hill. It had a floor smooth enough for dancing. Seats lined one side of it and the other side was open with a view of the coast. Summer trippers rested here after climbing the hill and children from the village gathered to play in the afternoons, lining up for *Nuts in May*, *Tom Tiddler's Ground* or *Oranges and Lemons*. Sometimes you could hear their chanting voices half a mile away. In the distance, they had a thin sadness like seabirds' cries.

Maureen, who didn't want Timmy Kelly to think she was coming for him, decided to bring the kid along to join in the games. Then she could stay on when the dancers started drifting in towards teatime. But the kid was shy.

'Call her Jane,' said Mrs Connors. '"Kid" is for goats.'

Jane wouldn't go out her own gate. No! She pulled away from Maureen and ran to fondle her cat, a spoiled thing like herself but afraid of nobody. Maureen could see that it had never been kicked and its impudence annoyed her. Jane rubbed her face in the fur of its belly and said she didn't want to go out. 'Ponger doesn't want me to.'

'You'll get fleas on your face,' Maureen warned. 'They'll jump in your mouth.'

'Take things slowly,' Mrs Connors advised her. 'Maybe if she gets used to you, she'll go out later.'

She sighed, then went indoors to work on her book. Maureen wondered how you made one. Did you attach the pages with glue or use a needle and thread? What you needed most, Mammy had explained, was peace and quiet – which was where Maureen came in. If she couldn't get the noisy brat away from the house, she might lose this job – and jobs were scarce.

'Play in the garden for a bit.' Mrs Connors was at her window. 'Jane, show Maureen your swing!'

So the two took a few rides on that. But the little girl's voice was loud and when Maureen tried swinging with the cat on her lap, Jane shouted, 'He doesn't like it. Put him down!'

In no time the mother was back out, smiling and explaining that the cat mustn't be teased.

Not even the cat? Maureen felt that she was being teased herself.

'Here's an idea,' said Mrs. Connors. 'I'll give you money for ice-cream. Jane will surely go out for that.'

So out they went and bought two tuppenny Hughes Bros wafers at the village shop. Then, licking them, set off up the hill towards the shelter guided by the chant: 'The Farmer wants a Wife / The Wife wants a child / The child wants a nurse / The nurse wants a dog . . .' And on and on, everyone wanting and getting and pairing off and lining up together so that Maureen, who had only left school that morning, felt a pinch of loneliness as if she were the last one in a playground whom no one had picked for their side.

Of course, Jane had never come to the shelter. Children from houses like hers didn't. Only villagers. *She* was the odd man out here, thought Maureen, feeling pleased as the small girl stared about.

And now – for the afternoon was nearly over – an accordion struck up. Timmy Kelly played a jig and dancers were soon tapping the cement, toing and froing on quick, flying feet. So far they were only children, but soon the bigger ones would join in and later it would be all slow foxtrots and fellows getting a chance to hold girls in their arms. Evenings at this time of year stayed bright until after ten.

'Look,' Maureen instructed Jane, 'this is how you do it. Point your toe.' And, before she knew it, she was dancing with the small kids, laughing at her boldness and catching the accordionist's eye.

Perhaps she lost track of time as the medley of tunes went on and on, for someone had to catch her by the elbow.

'That kid you come with went off! Disappeared!'

'Where? She was here a minute ago.'

'Ran after a cat. Said it was her own cat that followed her here. You should have kept your eye on her.'

'She could run under a bus,' said a girl, 'below on the road. Be flattened.'

People were enjoying their disapproval and Maureen, panicking, could just hear how they'd report an accident to Mrs Connors – but there hadn't been an accident! 'Jane,' she called nervously and ran around the back of the shelter, then downhill through a dark thicket. 'Ja-ane!' Several others joined in and soon the name. 'Ja-ane!' was echoing up and down the hill.

Sticking out from one of the thickets Maureen saw two striped trousered legs with wrapped around them the mottled, pink and white calves of her sister, Meg. Apart from the mottling, she would know Meg's old shoes anywhere. Then the pair moved and she saw that the man was her Dad. Why did they have to come here? Why here? The others will surely see them. 'Don't let them!' she entreated, 'damn you, God!' She felt batted by anxiety between blasphemy and prayer.

'Jane,' shouted someone above her head. Then: 'Here she is, Maureen. We've found her! Where's Maureen gone now? Mau – reen!'

Out she shot like a cuckoo-clock cuckoo. 'I'm coming!' she cried. 'I'm coming!' And began toiling up the slope.

Above her – what had he seen? – stood Timmy Kelly and behind him, in a group of children, was Jane holding her cat against her shoulder. Ponger. His black, feathery tail hung down past her knees. She'd had to go find him, she was telling the others. He'd come out after her then been scared by a dog and she'd been afraid he'd run off for good. Cats did that, she explained. Prim. Frowning. An old-fashioned child! Timmy Kelly winked at Maureen who looked away. Another time she would have winked back . . . She tried not to remember those mottled legs. Meg always stayed home in the evenings and had spent so much time in front of the open fire that the honeycomb of red heat marks had got permanent. Sometimes she lifted her skirt to let the warmth reach under it. Mammy should have beaten decency into her while she could.

'I'm going home,' said Jane.

Timmy Kelly was still perched on his rock like the king of the castle. Below him lay the thicket and it seemed to Maureen that he kept looking down at – what? She couldn't leave now.

'Don't look,' she wanted to shout. But that would only make things worse. If only she could distract him.

Suddenly, angrily, she jerked the creature from Jane's arms. Jane, in a shock of amazement, batted the air but could not get close and Timmy Kelly's mouth fell open as Maureen, mad with wicked triumph, whirled the cat round and round and round again in a dance of fierce, solitary freedom. As she twirled, everything blurred, and when she collapsed and let go of the cat, which staggered off, she was too blind to see the look on the faces reforming around her like reflections in a troubled pond.

'She's gone again,' she heard them say. 'The little girl's run home. She's in a state! She's sure to run across the road. Under a car! You'd best go after her.'

Panting, she ran down the hill, caught the weeping child's hand and saw her safely across the road to her own gate.

She left her there. She'd surely lost the job anyway, so why let Mrs Connors eat the face off her as well? When she'd seen the child walk down her path and in her own door, Maureen started back up the hill. The music had not begun again, which meant that they must be ballyragging her behind her back. Handing out blame was their greatest glee.

The word stopped her. Glee was the very feeling which was fading in her and which she would have liked to hold onto for fear of what might take its place. She felt a great yawning inside her.

Then she heard the accordion. Timmy Kelly was playing one of Moore's Melodies. 'The Last Rose of Summer'! Sad, melting, drawn-out sounds pierced and made her cry. Only it wasn't

Timmy playing it at all, but someone else, for here he was, waiting for her, on the path.

'Poor little wild cat,' he put his arms around her. 'You're crying. Don't. Come on,' he coaxed, pulling her behind some bushes, 'in here where they won't see me give you a kiss. You're a mad little cat, aren't you? A wild, bad little one? I think I'm going to have to swing you round by the tail!'

KISS ME HARDY

Beryl Bainbridge

Beryl Bainbridge has written thirteen novels, two works of non-fiction and five television plays. She won the *Guardian* Fiction Prize for *The Bottle Factory Outing* and the Whitbread Prize for *Injury Time*. *An Awfully Big Adventure* was shortlisted for the Booker Prize in 1990. She is now at work on her new novel.

KISS ME HARDY was commissioned with Traveller Magazine and broadcast on Radio 4. It was read by the author.

KISS ME HARDY

Hardy Roget and his friend had been booked onto the cruise two months before; it seemed foolish to abandon the whole idea just because one of them had died in the meantime. There was also a penalty clause, although Roget's agent said the shipping company would never hold him to it. Not in the circumstances; it wouldn't be good publicity. Besides, now that the funeral was six weeks into the past, Damien Cartwright had stopped asking him along to the BBC club for a drink and Barbie Cartwright no longer phoned up to see if he needed a spot of shopping. And he was sick to death of eating alone.

The ship sailed from Southampton. No sooner had he entered the embarkation lounge than a tall woman in a hat waved at him. He fluttered his hand in response; it was a reflex action. Since appearing twice a week for four months, two years before, in a popular television series he had become used to people thinking they knew him. Usually, unless drunk or young, they darted towards him, realised in mid-stride he was merely a character on the box, and turned heel. The woman in the hat kept on course. She was middle-aged and her eyes were bold. 'Hardy Roget,' she said. 'Such a pleasure. I've been so looking forward to meeting you.'

'How kind,' murmured Roget. He didn't meet many people who actually knew his name, and certainly none who pronounced it as though he had compiled the Thesaurus.

'I booked immediately I read you were giving a lecture.'

'It's not a lecture,' he corrected. 'There's some sort of script-writing course for beginners . . . I'm merely on hand to act out the finished results.'

'I wouldn't miss it for worlds. Why don't you buy me a drink?'

Her name, she said, was Sheila Drummond. This was her third cruise, only this time she was travelling with Fiona, her tennis-club friend of twenty years. For all of ten minutes he enjoyed her company, felt flattered she had sought him out. They sat on stools at the bar and her crossed knee shone. She was very confident, very amusing. Nor did she pester him with inane questions about the fictional goings-on of Dr Gregory and Sister Middlechap. She didn't say she'd last seen him enclosed in black bin-liners on the sluice floor of that hospital in Newcastle. Instead, she spoke about the recession and how her husband, John, distrusted the notion of the so-called 'green shoots' of recovery. John wasn't accompanying her because it wouldn't look good, he nipping off to enjoy himself while business forecasts were so dreadfully bleak. Then she said. 'You know how it is with some men . . . they grow old before their time . . . any excuse will do,' and she pressed the palm of her hand against the breast of Roget's suit.

Immediately, he felt uncomfortable; he nodded and smiled but his mouth tightened. Quite apart from other things, if he wasn't careful she'd be expecting him to buy her drinks for the duration of the voyage. Struggling up the gangplank he managed to give her the slip. He found himself ahead of two girls, one of whom cried out, 'I don't believe this. Pinch me. Is it really happening?'

His cabin steward was called Gary. 'I'm at your beck and call,' he assured Roget. 'Should you need anything, just press the button by the bed and I'll whizz in like a bumble-bee.' He placed Roget's suitcase on the bed and stroked its top. Roget handed him a tenner. He could scarcely afford it, but theatrical gestures were second nature to him.

'Glad to see you escaped your plastic bags,' Gary quipped.

That evening there was the usual round of cocktail parties given by the Captain, the first held at five o'clock and the most prestigious one at seven-thirty. Roget was depressed that he had been asked for the six o'clock 'do', along with thirty-five members of a wine-tasting club, a group of senior managers from Sainsbury's and a young honeymoon couple who had won some sort of competition. 'It was ever so easy,' the bride told the senior managers. 'You just had to tick what was the most important thing, money, love, or a sense of humour.'

'She put love,' said the bridegroom, at which everyone listening roared with laughter.

At dinner, Roget was placed at a round table with the tutor of the script-writing course, a man and a woman who only opened their mouths to eat, and the two young girls – one from the Midlands and one from Cardiff. During the meal, Roget gathered that they had both entered a writing competition and come joint first out of five hundred entries. Their prize was a week's cruise and free tutoring on the script-writing course. 'I still can't believe it,' squealed the girl from the Midlands. 'I have to keep pinching myself.' The tutor stirred his soup round and round and emptied a bottle of red wine in under five minutes.

When the girls had gone – they'd heard there was a disco on a lower deck – he said, 'I hate this sort of thing. I'm a poet, for God's sake.' Lighting a cigarette he blew smoke across the table. The woman opposite began to cough.

'Christ,' said the tutor, glaring at the couple. When they too had left he confided gloomily to Roget, 'Tomorrow morning, half a dozen matrons from the Home Counties will sign up, wear us out for two hours asking damn fool questions about writing for *Emmerdale Farm* and then never be seen again.'

'Surely I won't be needed right at the beginning,' said Roget. He had no intention of putting in an appearance a moment before it was absolutely necessary; he had been employed to speak lines, not hang around watching them being written.

He pencilled his cabin number on the back of the menu and suggested the tutor should give him a tinkle in a day or two.

'But I'll see you at meals,' protested the tutor. 'They've allotted us the same table.'

'Possibly,' said Roget, 'but I wouldn't count on it. I'm afraid I have a wasting disease, and don't feel frightfully gregarious.'

'Well, sod you,' said the tutor, pouring himself another glass of wine.

Roget went up on deck and sat on a bench, staring out into the darkness. From the deck below he could hear music; in his mind he saw a glittering saxophone. He was cross

with himself for inventing something so debilitating as wasting. Once the tutor had sobered up he was bound, out of
remorse, to pass the information onto the entire script-writing
course. I shall be forced to elaborate, thought Roget. I shall
either have to faint a lot or be seen dragging myself up
the stairways. He was just wondering if wasting necessarily
precluded a healthy appetite, when a voice said, 'There you
are' and Sheila Drummond plonked herself down beside him.
He shifted sideways and hoped she thought he was just
making room.

'It's not like being on a boat, is it?' she asked. 'It doesn't go
up and down, and you can't open the portholes.'

'Ship,' he corrected her. 'Not boat.'

They had quite a pleasant conversation. At one point he almost
wondered whether she wasn't cleverer than she appeared. He
had explained to her, on her insistence, how you could build
up character when acting out a part, add little mannerisms,
inflections of speech, and she said, 'Wouldn't you get closer
to the real person if you cut all that out?'

Then she asked him if he lived alone. 'Recently, yes,' he
admitted. 'I have just buried my friend.' In the last few weeks,
having uttered the same sentence many times, he had grown
used to faces suddenly expressing assumed concern. Of course,
he couldn't see her face, but there was no mistaking the tone of
her voice. She said, 'I hope nobody saw you,' and he laughed in
spite of himself.

He told her that Francis had played the saxophone. They
hadn't been lovers for five years. Health problems, mostly: 'It
was difficult adapting to being just friends.'

'Who wants men and women to be friends?' she said. 'One
might as well buy a dog.'

She had obviously misunderstood him and he wasn't liberated
enough to say outright that his friend's name was spelt with
an 'i' rather than an 'e'. It was then, to protect himself from
her possible advances and as a preparation for the outcome of
the script-writing course, that he told her there was someone
waiting for him in Gibraltar; someone he'd corresponded with
for two years.

'What does she do?' He thought he detected disappointment in her voice.

'She doesn't do anything. She has private means.'

After a pause, Sheila Drummond asked, 'What does she look like?'

'Small,' he replied, 'with auburn hair. And she has a slight limp. Nothing really wrong, just a war injury in her childhood. Her father was in command of a battery and during a naval battle a shell fell on the barracks and she received a piece of shrapnel in the ball of her foot.'

'How dreadful,' said Sheila Drummond. 'I didn't know soldiers were allowed to have their wives and children living with them. Not in wartime.'

'Their family has been living on the Rock for generations,' he said hastily. 'An ancestor served under Nelson and is buried in Trafalgar cemetery, just outside Gibraltar's Southport Gates.'

They talked about Nelson for several minutes, whether it was likely that he had actually cried out 'Kiss me, Hardy' before expiring, and then Sheila Drummond complained of feeling chilly. Before returning to his cabin, Roget went to B deck to see if he could find a booklet on the history of Gibraltar, but the library was closed.

For the following two days he managed to avoid both the tutor and Sheila Drummond. He took breakfast in his cabin and ate lunch and dinner in the Club Lido. He read a book on the six wives of Henry VIII from cover to cover and then started it again. It was quite safe to lurk about aft of the upper deck; sea breezes played havoc with a woman's hair. It was not until Wednesday night, as he was returning from the synagogue on Three deck, that he saw her again. She was with her friend Fiona. 'You've been hiding,' she said. He was forced to escort both of them to the Grand Lounge and buy them a drink. It was quite obvious it wasn't their first one of the evening.

'It's the great day, tomorrow, isn't it?' said Sheila Drummond. He was puzzled. 'You'll be seeing your friend, won't you? Barbara, wasn't it?'

'No,' Roget said. 'Anne . . . Anne Cleaves.'

Sheila Drummond told Fiona that it was a real love story.

There might even be wedding bells. Fiona suggested he bring Anne back on board for supper. There was nowhere decent to eat in Gibraltar. He insisted it was out of the question. Anne wasn't very well: 'Actually, she has a wasting disease. It's only a matter of time.'

'I thought she just had a bit of cannon ball in her foot,' said Sheila Drummond.

The next morning the ship docked at Gibraltar. He was on deck as early as possible. Even so, Sheila Drummond waylaid him. 'I'm so sorry,' she said. 'I'm afraid Fiona and I behaved very badly last night. It was the drink, you know,' and she pressed his hand and gave a sad, apologetic smile.

He spent the entire day sightseeing. Walking up Engineer's Road to the Upper Rock he was choked by the exhaust fumes of cars and coaches stuttering their way to St Michael's Cave. He climbed even higher, until he reached the observation platform on the lip of the North Face. It was raining and the view of Catalan Bay was lost in drizzle. Retracing his steps down Queen's Road he saw three apes pelting another smaller one with stones. All four animals were hideously ugly, with callused feet and armpits denuded of hair. Their victim was gnashing its teeth and leaping frantically up and down the slope. I know how it feels, thought Roget, and, depressed, he walked back down to the harbour.

At seven o'clock that evening, as he was going towards the Club Lido, Sheila Drummond leapt out at him from the book shop.

'Anne's awfully nice.'

He stared at her.

'And she looks the picture of health. She's in the Grand Lounge with Fiona.'

He wasn't at all surprised, though his heart was still hammering, to find Fiona sitting on her own. He was damned if he was going to let them think he couldn't take a joke. The band was playing an old-time waltz. Numerous couples of advanced years were gliding stiffly about the dance floor.

'Hello,' he shouted. 'Had a good day?'

'So, so,' she replied. 'Anne's gone to the loo. She won't be long.'

Roget ordered a double scotch. He hadn't eaten all day and immediately felt amused and uplifted. 'I saw those God-forsaken apes,' he said, and gave a mock shudder.

The waltz over, the band struck up a brisk fox-trot. Several ladies approached Roget and demanded a dance. It was Ladies Night and perfectly acceptable. He explained he was already spoken for, that he was waiting for someone.

It was while he was trying to catch the waiter's eye to order another drink that he saw a small, rotund woman threading her way between the tables. She had very rosy cheeks, wore a blue bow in her red curls and was well into middle age.

'Hardy,' she said. 'Please dance with me. It's our tune, remember?'

She wouldn't let him go. She slipped one hand from his shoulder to his neck and caressed his hair; she pressed her stout body to his. She said she was sorry about Francis but that she would look after him and he was to put the past behind him. And he could give up his silly acting career. After all, she had enough money for both of them.

As they limped round the floor he caught glimpses of Sheila Drummond's face. She was openly laughing.

'I do think we ought to sit down,' he said. 'The doctor warned any exertion might prove fatal.'

'Did he?' she said, and clung the closer to him.

The body was taken ashore with almost indecent haste. Roget explained to the police that he had never set eyes on Anne Cleaves until she button-holed him at the Ladies Night. She had said something to him when she lay dying in his arms, and used his name, but he hadn't caught anything else.

Sheila Drummond told Fiona it was possibly 'Kiss me, Hardy', and felt ashamed.

THE PACT
Joyce Carol Oates

Joyce Carol Oates is the author of a number of novels and story collections, essays and plays. Among her various literary honours she has a Continuing Achievement Award in the O. Henry Prize Stories series. She lives in Princeton, New Jersey.

THE PACT was first broadcast on Radio 3.

THE PACT

And then, this fiercely bright January midday in Acapulco, in a square popular with tourists, after how many years, Stearns sights Stoner.

Freezing dead in his tracks. And that lurch to his heart, the adrenalin rush. Tears smarting his eyes.

Having many times, how many times he could not guess, seen Stoner in the intervening years – imagined he'd seen Stoner. But never until this moment has it truly been Stoner.

Matthew Stoner, sitting in an outdoor café, beneath a striped umbrella, reading a newspaper and sipping a drink. Unmistakable. Though a mature-youngish man now, with a receding hairline, something fleshy in the jowls, yet a boyish face; an odd expression of anticipation about the mouth. He wears an expensive seersucker sport coat and a striped shirt raffishly open at the neck. His skin is as Stearns remembers – thin, pink, translucent, the kind that does not tan, only burns – yet he looks healthy, confident, supremely American.

A man who knows not only who he is but how much he is worth.

Stearns tugs at the rim of his grimy panama hat and squints through his blue-tinted glasses, staring at his old friend. He is perhaps fifteen feet from the Formica-topped table at which Matthew Stoner is sitting alone. His heartbeat is so rapid it threatens to spill over into something dazzling as molten gold. Amid the steady stream of pedestrians Stearns' stillness calls attention to him so that, after a minute, Matthew Stoner glances up.

Their eyes lock – fleetingly. Stoner returns to his newspaper which Stearns recognizes, even at this distance, as the *New York Times*. He doesn't remember, Stearns thinks. A furious choked elation sweeps over him. Of course, he doesn't remember. I've done the remembering for us both.

And then, so casually, as if he has rehearsed this meeting many times, and is fully in control, Stearns approaches Stoner and says, smiling, 'Hello he*llo*. It *is* you,' and Stoner looks up again, now narrowing his eyes, his expression tight and guarded, for of course he's a well-to-do American tourist and has been approached numerous times in this Mexican resort city by beggars and persons of questionable motives, and ventures to say, 'Yes? Are you speaking to me?' and Stearns almost laughs aloud, his old friend's tone is so . . . dignified. So adult.

'To whom else would I be speaking, Matthew, if I could speak to you?'

Lightly ironic, not at all accusing. And Stearns' own boyish smile, a bit lost inside his ragged grey-streaked beard, but, he's sure, disarming. So his old friend stares at him with widened blank eyes – eyes too shadowed by tinted lenses, in Stoner's case a more conventional aqua-green. And, when Stearns extends his hand for a handshake, American-brisk and no-nonsense, Stoner seems not to see the hand.

Is it because it's a hand of gnawed-looking knuckles, a hand of dirt-blackened nails, a hand of fingers glittering with cheap-bejewelled rings? Or because Stearns' baggy nylon shirt is such a peculiar colour, a sort of soiled Day-Glo puce? – and the long sleeves so long?

But, no: Stoner is staring only at Stearns' eyes.

He knows me, Stearns thinks. But of course there's the game to be played.

'Have we met?' Matthew Stoner asks, coolly civil, and Stearns says, his smile harder, 'Don't tell me you don't remember me, Matthew!' and Stoner says, stammering, 'Why, I – Matthew *is* my name –' and Stearns laughs, 'Of course Matthew is your name: Matthew Stoner. You wouldn't allow anyone to call you Matt.'

Stoner's cheeks have pinkened with blood as if they've been slapped. He's blinking rapidly. Wondering, Stearns thinks, how he can escape.

'I – almost – can remember your name,' Stoner says, 'you were in my high school class – Union City, PA? – class of 1976?'

'Yes,' says Stearns, 'but I didn't graduate.'

'Perry! Your name is Perry.'

'No, but that's close.'

'Graham?'

Stearns laughs, enjoying this. 'No, but that's close.'

'Michael? – I mean, Matthew.'

'You're Matthew.'

'Then – you're Michael.'

'Well,' says Stearns, pressing forward into the shade of the umbrella, hand extended so that, now, Stoner can't *not* shake hands with him, 'one of us has to be, right?'

So they shake hands. And how unnaturally cool and clammy-damp is Matthew Stoner's handshake.

Other patrons in the café, mainly American tourists, are glancing in their direction. Stearns, who makes it a point to study such fellow citizens, with the detachment of a cultural anthropologist, ignores them now. Isn't his old friend going to invite him to join him at the table? – join him in a drink? Stearns pulls out a chair and sits down. So the issue's decided.

'Michael Stearns,' he says expansively, tipping the brim of his panama hat whose sweat-grimy band fits his head loosely as a turban, '– "Mikey".'

Stoner's alarmed eyes take in Stearns' wispy beard, the thin sly bloodless lips, the neon-nylon shirt, the exotic 'native' rings on the fingers. Quickly he says, 'I wish I had time to talk, but I – I was just about ready to leave – I mean, I'm waiting for someone and we're leaving . . .' His voice trails off forlornly. Stearns just smiles. Close by, a motorbike backfires: everyone in the café excepting Stearns and Stoner turns to look.

'It would be sad, it might almost qualify as tragic, for us to meet like this, by chance,' Stearns says, and this too with the sonorous, measured air of rehearsed speech, 'but not to talk. Not to have time to talk. Matthew.'

'But I – I really don't – have time. I was just . . .'

In his agitation Matthew has pushed his drink, so luridly

scarlet, away from him, only half-consumed; he has folded up his *New York Times* carelessly, as if preparing to discard it. Stearns watches, bemused.

In other circumstances, Stearns would be alert to the possibility of picking up a discarded *Times* before it's cleared away as mere debris. No doubt it's this morning's edition, flown down from Los Angeles. Sold at the Hyatt, the Hilton, the Marriott, the Conquistador, high-rise luxury hotels overlooking the ocean. A walloping $2.00, American.

And there's the drink, too. Unfinished, left behind.

Except Stearns has too much pride, to stoop to that, in any circumstances.

Matthew Stoner asks awkwardly, across the yawning abyss of the sticky table-top, 'Are you, uh – vacationing here?' and Stearns says, 'Here? Acapulco? I couldn't afford it, I live here,' and Matthew Stoner's blank, not quite absorbing this, but pushing on gamely, 'What sort of – line of – work are you in?' his forehead creased as if in concentration, and Stearns laughs again, and says, 'I don't specialise, I think that's so limiting to the spirit, don't you?' Matthew nods. Blank and despairing. Then murmuring again he's so sorry he's about to leave, he's paid for his drink and he's waiting for someone – how delicately phrased, that someone! – to join him. They have to get back to their hotel because they're leaving, very early in the morning, seven o'clock, they have to pack – 'Sounds like you have an awful lot to pack,' Stearns says, 'starting the afternoon before. Wow.' Matthew Stoner smiles a faint, sick smile. And can't think of a single word to say.

So Stearns says, with an air of bright innocence and genuine curiosity, plucking at the straggly hairs of his beard, '*You're* on a vacation, eh? From where? Not Union City, PA, is it?' and Matthew shakes his head quickly no, 'Philadelphia, now,' and Stearns says, 'And with whom are you vacationing? – for whom are you waiting, even as we speak?' and Stoner swallows visibly, his eyes snatching at Stearns', murmuring, 'A, a, a – person. So I don't have time really to – talk.' Making a movement as if about to stand. But not standing. (Are his knees suddenly weak? Is there a band tightening around his chest?)

No, Matthew Stoner can't leave until Mikey Stearns releases him.

That's only justice, isn't it.

But Mikey Stearns, seeing there's no drink in the offing, nor even an apology for no drink, turns a trifle mean. Taking in the other's clothes, haircut, footware, digital platinum-band watch, grinning and shaking his head in awe, 'Wow, man. You seem to have done it, eh? After you vowed you never never would, you did?' so Stoner is forced to protest, 'I – really – don't understand what you're getting at,' and Stearns says, 'Crossed over. Made it. Become one of them. The ones we used to call the enemy. Remember?'

'No.'

'No?'

'I said no.'

'Well! What's your line of work? Let me guess. Corporate law? – investment banking? – medicine? – some 'challenging' and lucrative specialisation like – haematology? – gastroenterology?'

Stiffly Matthew says, 'Nephrology.'

'Neph-rology? What's that?'

'Kidneys.'

Kidneys! As if some tiny lever has been tripped in Mikey Stearns' brain, he begins laughing. A high-pitched breathless laughter, less an adult man's than an adolescent boy's. Hearing him, others in the café glance over, mildly curious. But Matthew Stoner does not join in. 'What's so God-damned funny?' he asks.

'*You*,' Stearns says. Wiping at his eyes beneath his blue-tinted glasses, readjusting the panama hat atop his head. 'You didn't recognise me at first, Matthew, did you? – I mean genuinely. That first glance. Wow. It was, like, metaphysical – the blank empty innocence of your blue eyes. *Sixteen years erased*.'

'Well, I – I had a lot of friends in high school – '

'But never a friend like Mikey Stearns. Yes?'

Matthew Stoner sits silent, though his mouth is working in a way that isn't very attractive. Like there's something in it, phlegm maybe, bile, he needs to spit out but dares not. In a

81

choked voice he murmurs, 'Why are you doing this to me, Michael?'

Stearns throws up his hands in a flamboyant gesture, like a stage comedian. As if this is the question he's been waiting for.

'Why, Matthew, who the Hell else is going to, if *I* don't?'

Stearns tells Stoner, calmly, even matter-of-factly, that he'd seen him, sighted him, hundreds of times, possibly thousands, these past sixteen years. 'Except, until now, it was never actually you. The North American continent is so vast.'

'I don't understand what – '

'Beginning in the hospital, I saw you. In the hall, or outside on the walks, you, Matthew, coming to see *me*, Mikey. Just a visit! A single visit!'

'It wasn't recommended that we see each other. Your parents – '

'Your parents! And you.'

Stoner says, licking his lips, 'Look, Michael, I – I don't owe you anything. I – was just a kid then.'

'We were just a kid.'

'My head was filled with so much shit . . .'

Stearns says, forcing Stoner to look at him, not allowing his gaze to slide away, 'No, not you, Matthew! You were the brains of the deal. You deciphered the "subliminal messages" in the music.'

'What music?'

'You composed the "farewell note".'

'What "farewell note"?'

It's at this point that Stearns, his bony hands clasped tight to keep them still, begins to lose his admirable control. 'What "farewell note"? – you're asking what "farewell note"? – oh this is fantastic! Sheer precipices of oblivion.'

Matthew Stoner says, frightened, 'You're not – anyone I know. Maybe you were once but you're not, now. You're a sick person. I can see it in your eyes, and I can – '

' – smell it on my breath: wetted ashes.'

As Matthew Stoner stares, Stearns unbuttons his shirt sleeves and now pulls them up to expose his pale, thin arms and the ghastly white scars on both forearms. On the interior of the arm, running from the wrist to the elbow, a half-dozen jagged scars on the left forearm and only two on the right, uneven and wavering. Saying calmly, 'We made a pact, Matthew, and you betrayed it. You betrayed us both.'

Stoner's face is flushed and mottled. He's staring at Stearns' arms as if he's about to be ill.

'Oh my God.'

'Well, what did you think? *Did* you think? At all?'

Matthew leans over clumsily, as if to tug at Stearns' sleeves, to pull them back down, to hide the terrible scars. Stearns eludes him. Lifting his mutilated arms to the sun, turning them, examining them, with a bemused, critical expression. 'Not a very pretty sight, I suppose. But I've lived with it so long, I can't quite see.'

Stearns pulls his sleeves back down, taking his time. Fussily buttoning the cuffs. Saying, 'We made a pact, Matthew. And it was a sacred pact, and you betrayed it, and all your life since then has been a betrayal, hasn't it? I'm the one secret you've never told *her*, aren't I?'

'"Her"?'

'You are married, aren't you?'

Matthew looks quickly around, blinking, rather blind-seeming, pushing his sunglasses against the bridge of his nose. For an instant he's touched by panic. Stearns can see the perspiration glittering on his face like infinitesimal bits of mica.

Matthew Stoner says, in a low, voice, 'She – my wife – has nothing to do with this.'

'Of course,' says Stearns, 'she doesn't even know.'

Stoner protests, 'I – we – were seventeen years old, Michael! Our heads were filled with shit. That sick, crazy music, drugs – '

'And our "worship", Matthew? What about that?'

'I didn't betray you, for Christ's sake, I saved you. I saved us both.'

'"Both"!' Stearns laughs derisively, but almost fondly. 'You were too terrified even to pick up the razor, let alone use it on yourself, after me.'

'God damn you, I saved us.'

'Is that how you remember it, when you remember it? "Saved us"!'

Stearns removes his hat and fans his heated face with it and returns it with a flourish to his head. He wonders if his old friend is surprised to see how thin his hair is, at the crown; how streaked with grey. What has happened to Mikey Stearns?

Stearns says, softly, 'And what about our "worship"? Have you forgotten that, too?'

Stoner's lips move. A convulsive twitch, the working of his mouth. As if he tastes something vile, poisonous.

'I – don't remember any "worship".'

'Don't you?'

'No. I said no.'

Stearns shakes his head in mock admiration. Or is it genuine admiration. Seeing the panic in his old friend's face, the boy's face trapped inside the other, damp widened eyes he remembers as blue, must take it on faith are blue; the thin cheeks inside the broad fleshy face. What has happened to Matthew Stoner? 'Well! Not only crossed over to join the enemy, you *are* the enemy, eh? Straight Caucasian male, professional class. Married, of course. Of course! And blessed with amnesia.'

Sitting very still, head lowered, Matthew Stoner is blinking and staring at the table-top. His lips are slack, his forehead is knotted. So softly Stearns almost can't hear over the noise of traffic, Matthew says, begs, 'Michael, let me go.'

Furious, Stearns says, 'What, you don't want us to meet? Don't want to introduce me to "Mrs Matthew Stoner"?'

Seeing the sick guilty look in Matthew's face Stearns feels, not rage, or not rage merely, but pity.

Pity! Him! This, he has not rehearsed, and could not have imagined.

He makes a sudden gesture, flicking flies away from the table, flippant, indifferent. 'Well. Too bad. We only just meet, and you have to leave. And there's no time. Shit, I'm sorry. But I understand.'

Sensing this alteration of mood, Stoner looks up immediately; like a dog, grown crafty through terror, he makes his move at once, pushing to his feet, eager to be gone. He's heavier than Stearns thought, thick in the torso, a high round little stomach pushing against his braided belt. The table tilts dangerously beneath the sudden weight of his elbows and the scarlet drink would capsize but for Stearns' swift intervention.

'Thank you, Michael! I appreciate it,' Matthew says, reaching out awkwardly to shake Stearns' hand, 'I – I really do,' a feeble smile, and the desperation to escape, not very flattering Stearns is thinking, but after all what had he expected?

Calling out, as Matthew backs away, 'What I'd hoped for was to forgive you. But – '

But already Matthew Stoner is out of earshot.

'– you didn't ask.'

With his habitual air of dignity, for he's accustomed, here in Acapulco, to being watched, Stearns gathers up the *New York Times* his friend has left behind; but he pointedly ignores the drink. Even if the frowning waiter were not approaching to clear the table, and to clear him away, Stearns would be ignoring the drink.

He leaves the outdoor café, newspaper under his arm. He moves unhurried along the street. How he will live out the remainder of his life, he has no idea. Where for so long he has rehearsed, now will he improvise?

LAST ONE OUT

Steve Dixon

Steve Dixon was born in Leeds. He has contributed poetry to various magazines and worked for M6 and Red Ladder Theatre Company. He has also been a director of the Arvon Foundation's Devon centre.

LAST ONE OUT was broadcast on Radio 4, read by John Evitts.

LAST ONE OUT

MINUTES OF THE MEETING OF THE DIRECTORS OF
JOSEPH DENTON & SONS (LIGHT ENGINEERING) LTD
– HELD 7th APRIL 1993.

PRESENT: None
APOLOGIES: None whatsoever
IN ATTENDANCE: Stuart Prynne, secretary.

In the absence of any of the Directors (or anybody else, in fact
– in the Boardroom, premises, or employ of Denton & Sons) it
was AGREED that Stuart Prynne be coopted to the Board.

At this point Stuart Prynne took the chair.

He took it from the skip out in the little car park (Directors' use
only), now empty, in which the last items of office furniture and
unsaleable junk were piled. It was AGREED that Stuart Prynne
should not risk giving himself a hernia by trying to get Mr Colin's
desk out of the skip, but should write these minutes on his knee.
Had it been a lighter, more modern desk, then perhaps . . . but
the great wooden slab at which three generations of Dentons
had transacted business dated from an age which expected less
movement in the Directors' furniture than in the Mountains of
Mourne. NOTED: This, according to the Receivers, was why Mr
Colin's desk ranked with the unsaleable junk.

Stuart Prynne took the chair to the centre the gutted
Boardroom. It clattered on the uncarpeted floor, and the clatter
echoed round the walls, stripped of the large, framed Denton
photos which had seemed almost like his own family album. The

chair squeaked when he sat down – as it had done, despite all oilings, for the past forty years. It was Stuart Prynne's own chair – swivel, dark green leather, worn to a crazed pattern, torn on the back support, left hand side – and he knew that squeak as well as he knew his wife's laugh, or the tick of the carriage clock on his mantel shelf at home.

ITEM 1: MINUTES OF THE LAST MEETING
Read, to the motes dancing in a harsh spring sunbeam, and approved (unusually) without carp or amendment. Thanks were expressed to S. Prynne for his concise and accurate recording.

ITEM 2: MATTERS ARISING
Under 'date of next meeting' S. Prynne raised the issue of the non-attendance of Directors today. He pointed out that this was the regular quarterly meeting, clearly entered in all relevant diaries. No indication of difficulties had been given when the date had been agreed in January. There was surely no excuse . . . And then the question of apologies – not one received! S. Prynne suggested that this was simply the last in a worrying series of oversights by Directors in recent months: the failure to consult with the Union over halving the workforce, straight after the January meeting (a decision not even alluded to at that meeting); the failure to make known the difficulties with the Barford order, until it had fallen through; the sale of valuable plant at knock-down prices; Mr Robert's sudden departure for a career in computer software and his surprising farewell bonus from the company; and most recently, the appearance of receivers, notices, and the piranha-like stripping of Denton Mill – home of high-grade engineering for over a century. S. Prynne's remarks were NOTED without comment.

ITEM 3: DUTIES OF S. PRYNNE UNTIL 5 p.m. 7th APRIL 1993, BEING THE TIME AND DATE OF EXPIRY OF HIS NOTICE
It had been AGREED that S. Prynne should remain in post for a day longer than the rest of the skeleton office staff who had

supervised the wind-up of the Company's affairs. This, as a mark of the Directors' trust in S. Prynne, and thanks for his long service to Denton & Sons. Stuart Prynne wished to put on record his appreciation of this request, but asked what he was supposed to do between now, 9.30 a.m., and 5 p.m. Every last scrap had been cleared; the phones were out; the power was off; and it was a cold day. (S. Prynne apologised for turning up to the Board Meeting in cap, scarf and gloves. Apologies accepted.) It was AGREED that S. Prynne should be available to deal with any last minute hitches, and to hand over the keys at 5 p.m. to the security firm who would then be responsible for the premises. In the interim, S. Prynne should make a thorough inspection of the Mill and offices to make sure that all was in order.

At this point, the meeting broke for refreshments. Patricia being otherwise engaged down at the DSS, trying to sort out her benefit entitlement, and there being no facilities in any case, Stuart Prynne offered round the small bottle of brandy, given to him by Mr Colin last week – the last time he had shown his face in the Mill his grandfather had built. The bottle still bore its gift tag – rendering thanks for past services and hoping for future happiness. It was warmly received on such a nippy morning. S. Prynne proposed a toast – 'To all our future happinesses!' Mr Colin, it was reported, was now acting as consultant to a large engineering concern based in Essex. S. Prynne informed the four walls that his own options were open at present.

Business resumed at 10.05 a.m., and it was AGREED that the remainder of the meeting should take the form of a tour of the premises (as agreed under Item 3) with S. Prynne minuting any items of special note.

ITEM 4: THE TOUR
4.1: THE GENERAL OFFICE
S. Prynne surveyed the stripped remains of his kingdom. Romans bearing fire and sword, Normans harrying the North, Russians in retreat could not have created a more complete wasteland. And yet, not everything could be obliterated. With

a smile S. Prynne NOTED a shape, like a ghost, or a trick of the light, traced on the wallpaper by the door to his own inner office. The difference between sunbleached paper, and paper hidden for years from the light had left the bright oblong imprint of Patricia's filing cabinet upon the wall. Patricia, 20+, fleet of hand, loud of mouth and clothes, sharp as a needle, much undervalued and underused as an office drudge. It was AGREED that if everyone got their deserts, her future should be brighter than her past. And yet she had wept when reading her letter of notice. Prynne liked her – NOTED it frankly. But it was not for her that a smile came to his face when he spotted the ghost on the wallpaper.

He went to the wall, and leaned against it as if leaning on top of Patricia's vanished filing cabinet. Of course, the wallpaper was different now. Denton's weren't known for over-attention to decor. But there had been a few changes in the last forty years. One thing wouldn't have changed, though. He knelt down and touched the bare floorboards, stirring a little dust. Yes, there it was. NOTED: one dark patch in the wood, as broad as a saucer-faded now, so that you wouldn't see it if you didn't know to look. And you certainly wouldn't know what it was. But Stuart Prynne knew. He informed anyone who was interested that this was a wine stain – cheap, red, vicious wine – he could still remember the smell. He straightened up and leaned on the wall again. He had been leaning in exactly this place when the wine had been spilled – December 20th 1955, Denton's Christmas party, old Mr Colin in the chair. And standing close to him, too close for comfort, had been Betty Green, then custodian of Patricia's filing cabinet.

Betty Green – 20+, fleet of hand, loud of mouth and clothes, in the style of her time, sharp as a needle and as undervalued as her nineties successor. For half an hour Stuart Prynne had found himself getting nearer and nearer to Betty as if by an attraction of physics, until at last they were crushed together in the corner by the filing cabinet. He was unsure, stuttering; she was laughing, in control. AGREED – if she wanted to she'd push past him with a cutting word, and that would be that. However, she didn't seem to want, at the moment – was content to make jokes about his massive quiff, about how he worked so hard he'd own the place one day (he was an invoice clerk at the time), about how he seemed to pay more attention to his chum Stan Mellors than to the girls, about the drink bringing him out of himself. She was content to watch him fumble for conversation, fumble to light her cigarette, and in doing so, knock her half glass of red plonk down his drainpipes and onto the carpet.

She hooted. He looked around quickly, but everyone else was so busy making noise and nonsense of their own that no one was paying the slightest attention. He stooped to pick up the wine glass – mercifully unbroken – and dab at the carpet with his pocket handkerchief. She was down there with him, pulling the carpet back. 'I'll smell this for weeks,' she said. The wine was soaking deep into the wood. Their heads bumped gently. Her fine hair brushed his cheek. He could smell her face powder, as she giggled and called him daft: 'Look at your strides. Come on, before it stains.' She took his hand and led him to the toilets.

ITEM 4.2: THE CORRIDOR

NOTED: on the door to the women's toilet, two small screw holes, near the top, much painted over, but never filled. FOR INFORMATION : this is where a small brass sign saying 'Ladies' used to be fixed. (In this visual age, it has been replaced by a cartoon figure in a skirt on a self-adhesive label.) In December 1955, Stuart Prynne had stared at the brass sign as Betty Green dragged him towards it. He was seized by the fear that she might actually pull him inside. Rather a lions' den than the Ladies! She didn't. 'Wait here a mo,' she said. And reappearing quickly with a wet hand towel, set to work on his trouser leg.

It was when she'd finished that finally, fleetingly, borne on a surge of hormones and alcohol, Stuart Prynne, 20+, had taken control. The corridor had been dark, as dark as on this last inspection. He'd held her by the waist and pulled her through the doors opposite onto . . .

ITEM 4.3: THE FACTORY FLOOR

FOR INFORMATION : up until last week outdated lathe benches
were bolted onto those studs in the concrete at this end. By
the corner of the first one, about here, Stuart Prynne, invoice
clerk, kissed Betty Green, filing clerk/telephonist, in the winter
of 1955. His tongue was all over the place. Somehow he'd
got hold of her bottom and was hanging on for dear life, and
amazingly she wasn't complaining. When at last they surfaced
for air, he felt dizzy; and she looked at her watch: 'I'm sorry – I
promised me mam I'd be back. I was just thinking of going when
you . . .' She pointed at his trousers, giggled, and was gone.

He didn't see her again until after Christmas, and then she just
smiled as if nothing had happened. For weeks, Stuart Prynne
was tormented – discussed Betty endlessly with Stan Mellors,
dispatch clerk. Until, in February, he went to the Mecca with
Stan and met Rosemary – the woman with whom he would
eventually produce three children, and whom he would see later
at the end of his last day at Denton's. It was at their wedding that
summer that the cap was put on the Betty Green story. Betty's
mate June had been talking to Stuart's mate Stan and had said.
'I don't 'alf envy the bride.' 'How so?' Stan had enquired. She'd
nodded towards Stuart, being pushed into place for a photo.
'He's supposed to be hot stuff.' Stan had asked her where
she'd got that from, and she'd said Betty – 'They had a snog at
Christmas,' June told him, 'and she said he was FABULOUS!'

Stan had waited a decent period after the honeymoon before
reporting this little conversation, but it stayed with Stuart for
the rest of his life.

FOR INFORMATION : Stuart Prynne has not much vanity in any
field, least of all with women. But each of us needs just a few
moments of glory to hang onto in life. He would like it minuting,
that, on this spot, near to these four studs, in December 1955,
for two or three minutes he, Stuart Prynne, kissed a girl and
was FABULOUS.

ITEM 5: ANY OTHER BUSINESS

Having completed his tour of Denton Mills, Stuart Prynne threw the meeting open. In the terrible silence that followed, the walls seemed as if they would burst around his head with all the moments of love, fear, disappointment, and joy they had contained since Joe Denton set on his first underpaid workforce three generations ago. But, despite a long pause, no further items of business were raised. Not a creak.

In conclusion, it was AGREED that these minutes be placed, together with Stuart Prynne's chair, in the company's one remaining filing system – the skip in the yard outside.

ITEM 6: DATE OF NEXT MEETING

Left blank.

Signed, Stuart Prynne,
7th April 1993.

THE GHOST WRITER

Julie Burchill

Julie Burchill has written two novels, two plays and five works of non-fiction. Her book of short stories, *Happy Hour*, will be published this year, and her new play *Gran* will be screened by the BBC. She is *The Sunday Times* film critic, and co-founder of the Modern Review.

THE GHOST WRITER was first broadcast on Radio 4, read by Haydn Gwynne.

THE GHOST WRITER

'Are you sure?' said her agent.

'As sure as I am that you're going to pick up the tab.' Rachel Gravelle poked her apple pie à la mode: 'It's weird about pie. If the stuff inside is so good, how come they have to cover it up?'

'That sounds like something Soho Brannigan would say.'

Val's blue eyes smiled at Rachel over the rim of her dessert wine glass. She looked like what she was; a Sloane off the rails, the last lady in publishing who seriously lunched – G and T's *before*, wine *with* and Beaumes de Venise *after*. It was her proud boast that in her fifteen years as a literary agent she had never once taken lunch at her desk. Under it, yes, but never at it.

Rachel stirred her coffee moodily: 'Exactly. I even talk like her now, or she talks like me. It's pretty creepy that I don't know which. One liners. Puns. She's a glutton for puns. She's taking over my life.'

'Isn't it more that she has a life of her own Rachie? The punters love her. The last three Soho Brannigan novels serialised on *Woman's Hour*. Two in the pipeline for TV.'

'You don't have to tell me, Val; you may get ten per cent of the bitch's booty, but I get ninety.' Rachel realised she had put six spoonfuls of sea salt into her coffee: 'But some things matter more than money.'

'Like keeping the boyfriend's approval?' Val looked around for a waiter, preferably one with a barrel round his neck.

'Like self-respect.' Rachel picked up her handbag and made vague I'm-outta-here movements. 'Val, I just feel I'm capable of so much more. And I've made up my mind. I'm killing that cow in the last reel of "Death By Chocolate" no matter what you say. And then I'm going to write my real novel.

'It's up to you. But Rachel . . .'
'Yes?'
'A lot of people won't like this.'

'You did great,' Gavin reassured her that night – and he wasn't just talking about her performance in bed. 'It's about time you started standing up for yourself. You let people walk all over you, Rachel, you really do. And don't listen to Mrs Ten Per Cent either, so long as she's got her crate of Petrus and her long weekend in Vail every month, she'd be happy to see you churning out hospital romances. Listen, while you're changing direction, why not change agents too? Actually, I've asked the old man to see you. He says the three of us can have lunch next week.'

She threw her arms around him; Gavin's agent was probably the hottest in London, with a list that read like a Booker Prize roll-call. 'That's great! How can I thank you?'

'We'll think of a way,' Gavin leered, pushing her onto her back. The funny thing was that he said it 'Ironically', with quotation marks around it. But he got what he wanted just the same.

It was that time of the night when you know that if you call someone – however close a friend they are – they will put you into that box marked '2 A.M. CALLER: DESPERATE, MAY BE DANGEROUS' and never really think of you in the same way again.

So calling someone – her usual ruse when stuck – was out. So was alcohol, because she'd finished it all.

Suddenly the words came to her. She sat down, unsteadily, and peered at the computer screen. Her fingers found the keys and typed in the words:

'It was all over. And as Soho Brannigan breathed her last, the latest Frederick's of Hollywood catalogue – not her life – flashed before her eyes. 'What a way to go,' she sighed – and was gone.'

Rachel sat back, pleased. Then peered at what she had written. But the words ran:

100

'Carefully, so as not to smudge her lipgloss, Soho Brannigan blew demurely down the barrel of her pearl-handled .45. "Didn't your momma ever tell you it was bad manners to send a lady mixed flowers?" The man on the bed jerked one more time, as if in agreement.'

'This isn't happening.' Rachel blinked, wiped her eyes, stood up and walked around the room very carefully, as if nursing a small sleeping baby or a terrible doubt. Then she sat down again and looked at the screen. Under the new ending were the words I'M NOT GOING. She closed her eyes.

I SAID I'M NOT GOING repeated the screen.

'This is not happening!'

IS TOO.

'Who are you?' Rachel asked.

I'M YOUR WORST NIGHTMARE. A PUPPET WITH ATTITUDE!

Not believing what she was doing, too spooked to actually say it, Rachel typed the awful words: ARE YOU SOHO BRANNIGAN?

GIVE THE GIRL A CRACKERJACK PENCIL!

'Before your time,' Rachel corrected her – it?

BUT NOT YOURS. YOU OLD TROUT, came the reply.

If she hadn't been so tranquillised on red wine and weariness, Rachel might have reacted more normally. But at getting on for three in the morning, it somehow seemed more manageable – if not exactly enjoyable – to conduct a dialogue with someone she had made up.

She typed in: WHY ARE YOU SO ANGRY?

THREE GUESSES! STARTS WITH A BANG, ENDS WITH A WHIMPER!

BECAUSE I WANT TO KILL YOU OFF?

OVER MY DEAD BODY!

'But you have to go.' It was quicker to speak now. 'I can't write detective novels any more. I have to do what I feel is right.'

AND WHAT MIGHT THAT BE, PRAY?

'My proper novel. *The Empty Room.*'

Something obscene came up on the screen.

'You've got a dirty mind, Soho.'

YOU GAVE IT TO ME. AND ANOTHER THING –

'What?'

WHY DID YOU HAVE TO GIVE ME A ST – ST – ST –

'Every detective has a gimmick,' Rachel explained.

GREAT. OTHER GUYS GET A LOLLIPOP OR A COOL OLD RAINCOAT OR A COWBOY HAT. BUT I GET A BLOODY ST – ST – ST –

There was a pause. Rachel could almost hear wheels turning. Then the screen got busy again.

CALL YOURSELF A FEMINIST! HUH!

Rachel felt sober, and tired, and crazy. It was not the most pleasant of combinations. 'What are you raving about now?'

DON'T WORRY, I KNOW YOUR GAME! LOOK HOW LONG ALLINGHAM STUCK WITH CAMPION. OR CHRISTIE WITH POIROT. OR SAYERS WITH WIMSEY. HOW LONG HAVE WE BEEN TOGETHER? – NOT EVEN FIVE LOUSY YEARS! I CAN SEE THROUGH YOU, THOUGH. I CAN READ YOU LIKE A BOOK. YOU'RE K-K-KILLING ME OFF BECAUSE I'M A WOMAN!

'You are not a woman! You are a character in a novel! A genre novel, at that! And soon, you're not even going to be one of those! Good night – sleep tight, or whatever you do!'

Rachel hit the computer's off switch, staggered into bed fully clothed and passed out. In the morning she was sick. A postcard from Stockholm, which she thought must be from her friend Kristina, said in the Swede's own hand GET WELL S-S-SOON, SWEETHEART.

'Rachel?' said Gavin testily. 'Testily,' she mused. It was a good word. It was mainly men who exhibited the trait, which was appropriate because it was typical of nasty things men did, like set you tests.

The cab was passing through Piccadilly Circus and Rachel was trying very hard not to scream: the neon, which to others touted soft drinks and camera film, said to her SM-SM SMALL WORLD, ISN'T IT?

'Soho,' she said.

'Yes, that's right!' The cab swung into Shaftesbury Avenue. 'We've been here a hundred times before. So what?'

'Sorry.' She wrenched herself back to Gavin's planet with a superhuman effort. 'I'm just nervous, I guess.'

'Rachel. How many times must I tell you? The two chapters

you showed me are exceptionally fine writing. Delicate. Fragile. As beautiful yet as tragic as a butterfly wriggling on a pin. The old man will love it. We're in for one very long, very lush, very expensive lunch.'

'It was filth,' said Gavin calmly, as a cab carried them away from their meeting only twelve minutes later. 'Pure filth, mind you, not tainted or adulterated in any way. Was it some sort of post-modernist prank, or something?'

'Gavin, I –' What could she say?: 'Gavin, the heroine of my detective novels, Soho Brannigan, is essentially dead but she won't lie down? And she can only act and move through words. And somehow she moved herself right into the opening chapters of my new book, my wriggling Cabbage White, and rewrote my tender, aching literary novel as schoolgirl smut. Gavin, what does your detached, analytical male intelligence make of that? Do you still love me?'

'Driver! Stop here, please.'

'Aren't you coming in?'

Gavin leaned across her to open the door. 'I think you've taken me in enough for one day.'

Rachel went straight into her office. The computer was off but the fax was on and its infernal bulletin was still spilling out, as if to welcome her home. She didn't bother, but turned the computer on straightaway and sat down before it.

'OK, you bitch. I'm back. What do you want?'

There was a hesitation. Then: JUST FOR THINGS TO BE THE WAY THEY WERE.

'Which was?'

YOU WRITING THOSE STORIES ABOUT ME. EVERYONE LOVING ME. WONDERING WHAT I'LL DO NEXT.

'I understand,' Rachel said. Could it be that women were educated to please others so thoroughly that if there were no man around they would mollify a piece of machinery, or coddle a computer, instead? If so, it was pretty grotesque. 'But don't you think it's getting a bit . . . samey, Soho? How many times can you fight the good fight against sexism and racism without once smearing your lipstick and still walk off with the babe of either sex at the end of the story? Face it; you modern girl detectives have become as weary a cliché as the old guys are, only in a quarter of the time. And our plots are nowhere as good as theirs.'

OUR BOOKS WOULDN'T BE SO SAMEY, IF YOU DIDN'T KEEP MAKING ME SAY 'SMORGASBORD' AND 'KISS THIS!'

'OK. Some of it's my fault. But I want to move on. Can't you understand that?'

DETECTIVE NOVELS ARE THE BALM OF GREAT MINDS.

'Who said that?'

CHURCHILL OR GRAHAM GREENE. I FORGET WHO. BUT YOU'RE ALWAYS SAYING IT TO INTERVIEWERS, THAT'S THE POINT I'M MAKING.

'Years ago.'

ONLY A SNOB AND A FOOL WOULD CONSIDER THE ENGLISH-SPEAKING LITERARY NOVEL TO BE IN A HEALTHIER STATE THAN THE DETECTIVE NOVEL.

'Who said that?'

YOU DID! DIMMO! NEW WOMAN, DECEMBER 1992!

Rachel decided to take a week off and not work at all. She turned off her fax and computer and avoided Piccadilly. But it didn't help. Street signs told her to G-G-GO HOME AND G-G-GET ON WITH IT! The Teletext in told her IT'S LATER THAN YOU THINK. An obliging skywriter scrawled across a sky as blue as Val's eyes: G-G-GET YOUR HEAD OUT OF THE C-C-CLOUDS AND YOUR NOSE TO THE GRINDSTONE, BABY!

'Don't you ever quit?'

NOPE, DON'T FORGET, YOU MADE ME THIS WAY. 'IRRESPONSIBLE, IRRE-SISTIBLE.' IT SAYS THAT ON THE BOARD OF *SOHO'S SMORGASBOARD*.

'This is silly.' Rachel pushed her chair back, balancing on two legs. 'We know too much about each other to fight. What do you want from me? To keep on writing the Soho Brannigan books until both of us are old biddies with bus passes? It beats jumping into a taxi and saying "Follow that car!" I'll give you that.'

There was a pause. Rachel knew by now that pauses signified embarrassment, or the nearest this friend would come to it.

THAT'S NOT WHAT I WANT.

'What, then?'

JUST DON'T KILL ME LIKE A DOG. LEAVE ME ALIVE, AT LEAST. THEN GO AND WRITE YOUR POXY NOVEL, *THE EMPTY ROOM!* BELIEVE ME, IT'LL BE MORE LIKE THE EMPTY BANK ACCOUNT BY THE TIME THE PUNTERS SEE IT. YOU'LL BE BACK.

'Thanks for your support.'

ONLY . . .

'What?'

LET ME WRITE IT WITH YOU.

'You?' Rachel lost her balance.

DO YOU REALLY THINK THAT ALL I WANT FROM MY ONE AND ONLY LIFE IS TO BE SOME PHONEY, STYLISED TO THE EYES GIRL DETECTIVE? THANK YOU VERY MUCH. A LOT YOU KNOW. I'VE GOT DREAMS. LIKE EVERYBODY ELSE.

'I never doubted it.' If she laughed, very quietly, could it hear her?

GO ON, LAUGH! I KNOW I'M A JOKE TO YOU. BUT I CAN WRITE IT WITH YOU. I CAN! JUST THINK WHILE YOU SLEEP, I CAN WRITE WHOLE CHAPTERS . . .

'That's what I'm afraid of.'

SUBJECT TO APPROVAL, NATURALLY.

'And if I say no?'

There was the longest pause yet.

THEN I'LL GO.

A slow sly smile ate Rachel's face and licked its lips. She opened her mouth to say, 'Go, then.' But instead, the phone rang.

'Rachel? Gavin. The old man called; he's prepared to overlook what happened last week as a small hiccup. The strain of writing serious fiction after five years of trash has obviously . . . taken its toll on you, shall we say.'

'Gavin. The only five years of trash that has taken its toll on me has been *you*.'

She put down the phone, went back to the computer. And very carefully, she typed in the words YOU'VE GOT A DEAL.

EDNA, BACK FROM AMERICA

Clare Boylan

Clare Boylan is the author of four novels and two books of stories. Her recent work includes a collection of writers on writing: *The Agony and the Ego*, and she is currently compiling *The Literary Companion to Cats*. She lives in County Kildare, Ireland.

EDNA, BACK FROM AMERICA was first broadcast on Radio 4, read by Diana Bishop.

EDNA, BACK FROM AMERICA

She went up to the water's edge and peered in. 'Go on,' she urged herself. 'Can't be much worse than a cold shower.' She lit a cigarette to feel something glowing other than the cabaret sign on the hotel behind her.

She remembered this place when she was ten years of age – a row of boarding houses in different colours fanned out along the prom like biscuits on a plate. When she had got off the train with her dad she'd thought that this was where it stopped at the end of the world. A donkey in a hat waited patiently to take them to the bottom of the beach. And then back. There wasn't anywhere else to go at the end of the world. All week they ate chips and went for donkey-rides and made pies out of the sand. He left her on her own at night but she didn't complain. She wanted to seem *soigné*. *Soigné* was a word he used. She couldn't believe it when the week came to an end. She saw the look of pity on his face, the rueful way his lips soothed the stem of his pipe. She was doing what he called a war dance. He took her back to Mum and Mr Boothroyd.

It was all changed now, cabaret hotels and karaoke lounges and hamburger palaces. Everything's different except me, she thought. I haven't changed since I was ten. Nobody wanted me then and nobody cares about me now. She sighed and threw away her cigarette. She began to scale the blue and gold railing. Behind her a crowd started to cheer.

She could hear car doors banging and a lot of excited noise as the cabaret hotel disgorged its patrons. 'Hell,' said June and she stepped down from the railing.

'Edna!' a woman kept calling out.

What would she do now? She hadn't the price of a hotel room.

'It is! It's Edna! Back from America!'

She turned around to discourage whoever was making the noise. A woman in a fur coat ran right up to her and plucked at her leather jacket with little fidgeting hands. 'Edna!' she cried, her eyes glittering with greed as if she was calling 'housey housey'.

'I'm not Edna,' June backed away.

The woman frowned. 'Don't you know me? Muriel!' She put out a hand and took it back again. 'Where's your things?'

'I've got nothing.'

'Your handbag?'

Sullenly June showed her hands in which only a pack of cigarettes was held. She shoved them back in her pockets.

The woman nodded. 'You've come as you went.' She seemed quite pleased. 'Everyone took it as proof when you left your handbag behind. No woman leaves without a handbag, they said. Not unless she's dead. You don't know Edna, I told them.'

'I'm not Edna,' June said. 'You've made a mistake.'

'No I haven't.' She wouldn't accept anything. 'Now look here . . . !' June began angrily, but her mind had gone blank. She stared wearily past the woman out to sea. Rain had started and the tide lapped delicately at the little mousey shards. Hell, it looked cold. If she had gone into the water and been fished out the following day there would be nothing to identify her. The woman called Muriel would turn up and swear that she was Edna. She began to laugh. Muriel watched her warily and then she too started to titter. 'You've not lost your sense of humour, Edna. You always were a tease. Now let's not stand here getting soaked to the skin when we could be home by the fire with a nice drop of scotch. You still like scotch, don't you?'

Here was one argument that June need not resist. 'Yes.'

They were settled around the Tudor-style fireplace with glasses of scotch in Muriel's mock-period house when Ted appeared.

'Ted! Look who's here!' Muriel challenged. A big man, uneasy in his successful suit, studied June seriously but without much hope, as if she was an examination paper.

'It's Edna!'

'Back from America!' the woman prompted.

'Edna!' He blew air through his teeth. 'America?' He studied her closely while he refuelled her glass. At last he nodded. 'You'd best stay here until things are sorted out.'

As she fell asleep in a room where everything was in matched shades of lavender, she wondered about Edna, what trick of personality she had to make herself so welcome to Ted and his wife while she, apparently with the same face, had no one. Maybe she and Edna were related. Funny how her dad had picked out this place. Perhaps he had a girlfriend there once and left her pregnant. Men were such bastards. Even Alastair. She'd accepted him without question, she'd loved him and nursed him through his illness. When he died there was only the house and its memories. Then his wife turned up. She never knew he'd been married. Alastair's small wealth had gone to her – a woman he had not seen in fifteen years. She was left with nothing. On the train on her way to this place where she had once been happy, a friendly youth talked to her and after he got off at his station she realised that he had taken her handbag. She was relieved in a way, for there was now no smallest point in carrying on another day.

'You've gone arty,' Muriel observed over breakfast.

Quickly June said that she hadn't gone anything, that she still wore the same style she had adopted in her student days. She had meant to leave early in the morning, to complete her mission at dawn on the deserted pier. Absurdly, she had slept it out. 'Look, I'm not your friend. You've been very kind, but I don't know you.'

The woman looked crestfallen. Then she began to cry. 'I'd know you anywhere.'

'I had nowhere to go,' June apologised. 'I hadn't any money.'

'Is that all?' The childish face dried in an instant. 'You always were too proud.' Muriel sat down heavily. 'Look love, I've got bad news and good. Your mum's passed on. I'm sorry. It's four years ago now. She left a bit of money for you.'

'How much?' June said.

'She didn't have much. Five thousand pounds. And of course there's her cottage.'

Later on, Muriel drove her to see the cottage, to show how she had tended the garden. It was a safe, and modest little house, guarded by lupins and red hot pokers. June, who was homeless, had an urge to move in right away. It was like a fairy story. She knew she must make the truth known to Muriel but she could not bear to break the spell.

It was Muriel's suggestion that she should revert to her old hairstyle. She allowed herself to be led to a dangerously homely looking establishment where a big woman called Beattie greeted her with wonder before holding her down like a sheep to be sheared. As she gripped and snipped, Beattie talked about the old days. The lives of women had not changed here as they had everywhere else. It was like a dance in which one changed partners for a brief number of years and when the music stopped, when you reached twenty-four or five, you stayed for the rest of your life with whatever partner happened to be opposite you. Terry had ended up with Renee, Joe and Sarah had a child who was backward, Bill Ferret, who used to look like Elvis, had gone bald and Sid and Sylvie weren't getting on too well.

'Sid and Sylvie,' June echoed distantly, thinking how well their names got on.

'Beattie,' Muriel warned.

They grew silent, watching each other in the mirror as Edna's face was summoned up under the scissors. Had Edna been abandoned by Sid in favour of Sylvie? Was that why she went all the way to America? Perhaps June and Edna had something in common after all. Beattie had cut her hair into a mound of uneven bangs that gave her an odd, rakish appearance. What would Alastair make of her now? She realised it didn't matter any more.

'There!' Beattie said at last. 'There's your old self for you. All you need now is your old accent. Fat lot of good that'll do you.'

As Muriel introduced her to Edna's old haunts, June discovered that the village hadn't really changed at all. It was the visitors to the pier that had altered, demanding an up-date of the town's single attraction – the donkey.

Alice Cranmer's fashion shop still had slips and lemon twinsets in the windows. Girls tried on pink lipstick in the chemist shop. A small dairy displayed faded windmills and postcards and sold damp ice-cream cones. June liked it. She knew that she must someday leave but for the moment she hung about Muriel watching for clues. 'You won't mind my saying, but I preferred your old style,' Muriel offered. Meekly she submitted to Mrs Harkins who pinned her into an assortment of close-fitting Doris Day dresses and costumes. She had her hair lightened and learned to walk on high-heeled sling-backs. When Muriel ceremoniously handed over Edna's old handbag, with its letters and photographs and shopping lists, June did not receive it as a final clue to the other woman's past, but as the lifting of a cloud of amnesia. Everyone accepted her. The one or two who had glanced at her suspiciously soon embraced her and she thought it was not because they had overcome their doubts but because they needed Edna. She was puzzled by the woman who had fled this simple, rich life. She felt entitled to take what Edna had thrown away.

It was a shock to discover that Edna had thrown away a husband and daughter.

She found the snapshot in Edna's handbag, a thin man with a solemn girl of eight or nine. 'Sid and Sylvie, Clipton Pier, 1983,' she read out from the pencilled caption on the back.

'You wouldn't recognise your little girl now,' Muriel shook her head. 'Sid hasn't changed much. Your husband never changes.'

June's attention was on the little girl, a child like herself who could not hold love. Edna had walked out on her own daughter. The thought of it brought tears to June's eyes.

'Maybe it's time you went home, love,' Muriel said gently. 'Ted and me don't want to rush you, but everyone's been notified. They're only waiting for you.'

On the way to the cottage she counted up the signs by which Sid might recognise her as an imposter. Had Edna a scar or mole? Was she eager or reluctant in bed. 'I'll make it work,' she determined. 'A month ago I had no one. Now I've got friends, a family, and a home. I'll make them want me even if they find out I'm not Edna.' She felt calm. It was Muriel who was nervous. 'About Sylvie,' she said at last. 'I should have told you. She's no better.'

'I'll take care of her,' June said quickly. She was used to sick people. She had taken care of Alastair.

Muriel sighed. 'They won't keep her in anywhere. Not even that mental place.

'Remember the time she set fire to the rabbit? She did it to a boy in the last home.'

June lit a cigarette. She drew on it as if draining a pond with a straw. 'Why couldn't Sid take care of Sylvie?'

Muriel looked uncomfortable. 'He's been inside again. Got in a fight with a man and left him in a very bad way. It's the drink, Edna. You know that. But he's promised he'll never lay a hand on *you* again. There was some around here that thought he'd done away with you. I never believed that. Well, I have to believe the best of my own brother. Anyway Sid'll behave with mother around. She's still a battle-axe, even though she's daft as a brush.'

'His mother?' June raked at her face and hair with her fingers as if a growth of cobwebs enclosed her.

'They threw her out of that Haven place now she's wetting. It's Alzheimer's.'

'Sid's your brother?' June disciplined her panic with reason. 'Then we're talking about your mother too. Why can't you take her?'

'I'm sorry, love. Ted won't have it. I didn't admit I was at my wits' end until you turned up.'

'Stop the car, Muriel,' June said. 'I'm not Edna.'

Muriel tittered excitedly. 'You've left that a bit late. They're all waiting for you back at the cottage!'

She tried the door, which was secured by a central locking device. 'Please let me out. I'm not Edna. My name's June Pritchard.'

The other woman took her eye off the road to sharply assess

ALL OVER THE PLACE

Michael Carson

Michael Carson comes from Wallasey, Merseyside. He worked abroad for twenty years, teaching English, and has written six novels and a book of stories; his recent novel is *Demolishing Babel*. He has also contributed over thirty short stories to BBC Radio.

ALL OVER THE PLACE was first broadcast on Radio 4, read by Jane Whittenshaw.

ALL OVER THE PLACE

A scrawl in radiant-blue ink on the right-hand corner of a battered school-desk – late of St Angela's Convent, Liverpool – now in the cellars of Humble Jumble, Chester:

> 'I've got to get out of this place if it's the last thing I ever do . . . Mary Lynch, June 17th 1966.'

Graffiti on a door, subsequently covered by three coats of white gloss paint, in the ladies' toilet at the Students' Union of Sheffield University:

> 'This isn't IT . . . is it? Mary Lynch on the occasion of her 21st bloody birthday. I've just drunk 21 halves of bitter and it's just not good enough!'

Notes on a Voluntary Services Overseas interview pad, now buried twenty-feet-deep in landfill below a Housing Estate in Basildon, Essex:

> 'Suggest rejection of candidate Mary Lynch, interviewed May 12th 1970. Reasons: overly romantic about life overseas; when asked whether politics was a topic open to discussion with host country nationals, "Oh, yes, I think so. Don't you?" Candidate smoked throughout interview . . . not a fitting cultural ambassador. Reject – unless no one can be found for Ulan Bator . . .'

Inscribed on a copy of Mao Tse Tung's *Little Red Book* which props up a table in the junior lecturers' staffroom at the University of Mongolia, Ulan Bator:

> 'Lies! Lies! I am SO disappointed in you, Chairman Mao. You know nothing about Mongolia . . . and you care less. This is no way to run a country! Mary Lynch, June 1972.'

Message on the back of a faded postcard, showing an orang-utan in evening-dress, which is still thumb-tacked to a wall of the nurses' room in a maternity ward at the St John the Evangelist hospital, Bombay:

'April 17th 1973. Hope and I finally made it to Shiraz on the bus. The ride from Kabul really did us in, but everyone was very kind. We may hang about here for a while. People say there are jobs for teachers. When I get the bread together, I'll kit out Hope in pink and get her christened, I promise. Thanks for all the TLC.'

Entry for May 14th 1973 from the baptismal register of the Christian Hospital Church, Isfahan, Iran. The book is now in the possession of Mullah Ali Hussain Gholpaigani at the Office of Religious Orthodoxy, Tehran:

'Name: Hope Lynch. Mother: Mary Lynch. Father: Hok Eng Lim.'

From the records of the Quick School of Languages – Isfahan School – dated September 17th 1975. Also in the possession of Mullah Ali Hussain Gholpaigani at the Office of Religious Orthodoxy.

Copy of memo to Mr Neville Quick, Quick School of Languages, Pepys Passage, London.
'Nev: Re previous memos, I have been forced to fire Mary Lynch from our teaching staff. I did this with some reluctance because she has been an efficient teacher, rather popular with students. However, her lack of tact on matters political has forced my hand. A man from the secret police demanded that I dismiss her. I had no alternative. Hands are tied, if you get my drift. No vacancy for little me in the Florence school, I suppose? Love to Felicity.'

Graffiti in Latin script – now covered by a Koranic text – under the thirty-three arch bridge in Isfahan, Iran:

'Opium is the opium of the people! Down with the Shah! M.L.'

Message dated December 27th 1975, from the autograph book of Kamal Erol, a guide at St Sophia's, Istanbul. The book lies buried with the body of its owner:

> 'Thanks for a wonderful trip. I have learnt a lot. I'd recommend you to anyone. You're the best! If you're ever in London, ring me. If I'm not there, someone who knows where I am will pass on the message. Love, Mary and Hope.'

Inscription carved in Persian calligraphy on a polished agate pendant, made in Isfahan, sold in the Istanbul bazaar and now in the possession of a retired American helicopter pilot residing in a mobile-home near Killeen, Oklahoma:

> 'My name is Hope . . .'

Last entry in a 1976 diary, bought in Cyprus and lost on a steamer to Alexandria . . . now at the bottom of the Mediterranean sea.

> 'February 27th: A warm wind blows. It bears Africa on its back. Hope keeps coughing . . .'

From an article in the *Guardian*, July 17th 1977, found under carpeting. Below the headline, 'Cairo: Dancing on one leg':

> 'To illustrate the point, Dr Akbar told me of an English woman who had brought her young daughter to his hospital. The child had been admitted but there was little anyone could do. She lingered for a week, then died and her body was taken away by the mother. "She seemed so poor," Dr Akbar said. "She shook her head when we asked her about her husband. We did not have the heart to ask her for money. I still wonder how she came to be here. We have not seen her again".'

Entry for October 23rd 1977, The Visitors' Book, British Club, Khartoum, Sudan:

> 'Mary Lynch, guest of Washington P. Booker.'

Envelope of a Christmas card postmarked 'Liverpool, December 2nd 1977', found by Hassan Ibn Abdullah in some reeds by the Nile and kept to the present, because of the Christmas stamp:

'Miss Mary Lynch,
c/o Washington P. Booker,
US Exploration and Drilling International,
Omdurman,
Sudan,
Africa.'

Envelope of a greetings card postmarked 'Liverpool, 6 June 1977' picked up from frozen tundra by an American Bald Eagle and woven into its nest – presently unoccupied – in the Mount Baez National Park, Alaska,

'Mary Lynch Booker,
US Exploration and Drilling International,
Whittier,
Alaska,
USA.'

Bankers draft for $2,000, shredded after encashment and subsequently burnt, made out to Dr Akbar of the Eisha Hospital, Cairo, Egypt.

Message written in snow – now melted and part of the Gulf of Alaska – January 1st 1979:

'Mary loves Washington.
Washington loves Mary.'

Hurried note scribbled in magi-marker on a double-door refrigerator in Dallas, Texas. The words were erased with a paper-towel, which was then discarded.

'Washo: It's no good. I can't hack it here. I'm leaving. Don't try to find me! Mary.'

Message in the Visitors' Book at D.H. Lawrence's mausoleum above Taos, New Mexico July 17th 1982:

'Well, all I can say is that you ended up exactly where you

deserved to be, DH! I've never seen anything as tasteless as this in all my born days! Serves you right for the way you put down women! Style but no substance. Now you've ended up with neither style nor substance! Frieda got the last laugh!

Mary Lynch'

Then:

'I agree with Mary! You're a disgrace, DH! All power to women!

Hilary Zeigen'

Message on an answering machine in London – a message not understood by the recipient.

'Hello, Mary! Are you there? It's Kamal Erol, your guide at St Sophia's. I'm here for seven days. I wanted to stay longer because there are problems at home. My brother has been taken away and I fear . . . anyway I am staying at the Regent's Palace Hotel. Please inform.'

Sign above a cake-'n'-book store in Hopi, Arizona, now converted into an Indian craft emporium, the sign painted over:

Hilary and Mary. Cakes Like Father Should Have Baked Books Like Father Would Have Burned

Visitors' Book of the Grand Canyon National Park (North Rim) for August 20th 1985:

'Wow! Hilary and Mary'

Note on a postcard of a Grand Canyon mule, used as bookmark in a library book from the Don Scotus Academy, Detroit, which is now in a bookshelf under 'Americana' at the Cinema Bookstore, Hay-on-Wye, Powys, Wales:

'Met a really great English chick called Mary. She seemed hot to trot but is with girlfriend who spits lemon juice at yours truly if I go anywhere go near! I'll tell you how I make out. Say "Hi!" to the guys at Nancy's. Rod.'

TELLING STORIES

From *The Grand Canyon Visitor's Bulletin* of August 29th 1985:

> 'The tragic death of Hilary Zeigen should be a warning to all hikers in the canyon . . .'

Fragment of a letter sent from Arizona to Liverpool, used as a spill to light a pipe, then discarded in the spill-holder – where it remains – just before the smoker expired:

> '. . . Rod's been a tower of strength. I don't know what I would have . . .'

Words spoken on the frozen porch of a house in a run-down neighbourhood of Detroit. The words steamed for a split second in the cold air:

> 'This could be Liverpool . . .'

Drawn with a finger on a bus window covered in condensation. Mexico, The Day of the Dead, 1985:

> 'Mongolia . . . Nepal . . . India . . . HOPE . . . Iran . . . Turkey . . . Egypt . . . NO HOPE . . . Sudan . . . Alaska . . . Arizona . . . Detroit . . . Mexico . . . Where?'

From a postcard sent from Rio, Brazil to Isfahan, Iran – not delivered due to statue of Christ in the background – and discarded in a sack at Tehran airport, the sack providing a pillow for Haji Ali Kardooni for the past few years. It reads:

> 'Shrove Tuesday, 1986. The Brazilians dance away the day while the Brits toss pancakes. I'll leave you to decide who does it better. Mary'

Written in biro on a napkin belonging to El Palacio de Sandwiches, Catamarca, Argentina. Received in payment for a Chilli Dog – and kept for reference inside his copy of *English for your World, Book 1* by Ignacio Powell, the owner of the establishment.

I am I'm not
You are You're not

He is He's not
She is She's not

Internal memorandum in the archives of the St Martin de Porres Free Hospital, Catamarca, Argentina:

'Re Mary Lynch. The patient was recovering from severe exhaustion but when routinely tested was found to be suffering from TB. We tried to locate an English-speaking counsellor who would inform the patient but, by the time this was done, the patient had discharged herself. Have made enquiries in the town but unable to trace her. Dr Pablo Muñoz, July 14th 1988.'

A burnt-down candle buried deep in a mountain-range of wax below a candle-holder in a Bolivian church. As it burnt, the woman who lit it stared into the flame repeating:

'Well, here we are then . . .'

British Airways ticket-stub: Santiago, Chile to London, Heathrow. The stub is in the side pocket of a shoulder-bag bought in Huancayo, Peru, 1989:

'Mary Lynch September 6th 1992 / Class: Economy / Status: OK'

From the supply-teachers' logbook of St Angela's Convent, Liverpool, May 6th 1993:

'Set work for 4B. See enclosed. Those two at the back tired me out. 5A were difficult. They said they did not understand the work set for them. I didn't either. It gave me a headache. I made them write an essay, entitled: "What I want to be when I grow up." I have left the results for you to mark. Mary Lynch.'

RHINO-SKIN

Moy McCrory

Moy McCrory was born in Liverpool. She has published three collections of short stories and a novel, *The Fading Shrine*. She is currently putting together another book of stories and now lives in Salisbury.

RHINO-SKIN was first broadcast on Radio 4, read by Dorien Thomas.

RHINO-SKIN

The eighteenth-century artist Pietro Longhi made two versions of a painting to commemorate the first showing of a rhinoceros in Venice in 1751. While these paintings are identical in composition some changes have been made to decoration and detail. A plainly dressed man smoking a pipe and a Dandy in a wig have been replaced by two sinister masked and veiled figures. In both paintings a man in a grey top coat waves the rhino's horn in his right hand and points. At first he appears unchanged.

When they brought the first rhinoceros to Venice they steered the cage along the Grand Canal on two flat boats lashed together with planks. Seeing the strange cargo, the noble dwellers of that exquisite republic thought at first it was some hoax.

A shivering winter now dripped towards a miserable Lent, but for these habitués of pleasure the grim months had been gilded into Carnevale. Familiar with excess they could be excused for thinking the rhinoceros was merely the result of bad wine, a remnant of cheese eaten late the previous evening, which caused them to recall some lurid sight, when masks and costume animated their nightmares and their desires.

The citizens blinked, rubbed their eyes, and when the apparition didn't vanish, they babbled delightedly that such a hideous misshapen beast would frighten honest people out of their wits. As word of the monstrous arrival spread, Venetians raced to see. So many people were drawn to the canal side, hanging from every available strut and prop and choking the walkways, that the guards had to be sent among them.

On the Rialto Bridge as the crush surged forward, shopkeepers slammed shutters, fearful of damage to goods and property. An old woman who remained with her basket thinking to make a killing, went down and was trampled by wooden shoe and slipper alike. Excitement drew no social division.

These people of the lagoon prided themselves on their sophistication. They couldn't be duped with cheap tricks. Having gorged on pleasure their jaded palates craved fresher delights. The last time a travelling showman had set up with feats of fire and a mind-reading display, he had been shown to be a fake. Yet women's shoes, descendants of the elevated zoccoli which had once picked across Saint Mark's, conveyed their wearers creepingly to buy his exlixir of youth. Those who wore sashes and yellow flowers to advertise their nightly activities fought hardest to obtain any potions, dreading the time their professional lives would be over. Money could always be made in Venice.

But the beast was no cheap fake. Some had already heard about this animal from the other side of the earth and its slow progression throughout Europe. Displayed for Crown Heads and commoners alike, causing a sensation wherever it went. The showman had toured it for ten years. Both he and beast were weary.

He approached the city in time for the close of Carnevale, for that last furious burst, when for two weeks possibilities erupted; a beggar might become a prince – a rich man pass for a pauper. It was a time when lives were exchanged, a time of masks, a time of deceit, when each woman could be beautiful, each fantasy fulfilled.

But the showman knew it was time to stop. He wondered if here, in the place of deception he might find rest, pass among folk not as a stranger but as a respected outsider; a patron of the arts perhaps.

When the rhinoceros went on display, as it had so many times before, pregnant women were advised to stay away lest the shock caused them to miscarry, and all women who were in their monthly flux were told, not unkindly, to wait, lest the creature got the smell of blood and came rutting.

Its horn was always the cause of lewd joking. The showman doubted there was anything he hadn't heard, but the Venetian capacity for novelty astounded him. Every day they thronged to see the rhinoceros, which, like a warrior bearing arms, defended itself from the assault of so many stares, for it kept its head down, visored like a knight.

In that first week hundreds passed through the viewing gallery. The showman was used to numbers peaking, then dropping off, but numbers increased as Venetians were irresistibly drawn to the grotesque. Carnevale sucked all into its maelstrom. A crazed drum, beat continuously like the heartbeat of the place, turning its citizens into one being. Pickpockets went through the crowds, knives were drawn and the showman counted his takings.

That year the rhino became the rage. Mask makers carved rhino faces and the showman, seeing further opportunity for sensation, forbade the wearing of these in the viewing gallery and posted a prohibition outside couched in heavy terms which stressed the danger of ignoring the warning. The animal was savage, and if roused – well, who knew?

In polite circles an admission of having not seen the rhinoceros was like admitting one had never travelled or read a book. A favourite topic of conversation became the witty things people told each other about the reactions of others, less sophisticated than themselves: 'My dears, he turned white completely. Then he began to shake. "The air," he said, holding a perfumed cloth to his nose, "the air isn't good," whereupon he fainted straight away.' The wigs bobbed with laughter. 'Fainted straight away!'

But the creature, as if sensing the end of the tour, did weaken. When it slept too long into the day, the showman poked the fleshy part of its faces with an iron bar where he could be sure it would catch. Sometimes he held flaming tapers to it, causing it to run in circles, stamping and shaking its massive head which made the audience scream with laughter, as if it were some great toy, dreamed up by the Almighty solely for their pleasure.

The animal was fading. It appeared less heavy, less dark in tone. Its eyes became translucent.

The showman considered. Venice with its soft corruption was ideal for him. He had found at last in this sickly, venal place a way of life to which he could become suited. Where everything and everyone could be bought, where all tastes could be catered for, and where he had money enough to satisfy his pleasures.

The showman was on nodding terms with many of his customers now. There was one fellow, always dressed in grey. He saw him everywhere he went – crossing the square, buying bread. He saw him when he least expected to. Always aloof, this grey man stood apart from the raucous crowds who poured in to laugh at the beast. The showman noticed that his response was different and thought the expression on his strange, sad face was compassion.

He was shocked when one afternoon this man approached him. He wanted to make an offer for the horn. That had been his interest after all. The showman's inclination was to refuse and see if the stranger would increase his price, but he was secretly pleased because he had seen how the animal was failing. Selling the horn would be a shrewd move; they wouldn't tour again.

'On its death then. You can have it.' But the stranger wasn't satisfied and argued that horn removed from a dead animal did not have the same potency, as horn from one still living.

'Potency? What potency do you mean?' But he knew.

The stranger assured him that he bought for a rich client, a septuagenarian of failing powers who had taken a new wife, not above fifteen and so needed all the assistance powdered horn might offer. Yet the showman felt he owed the animal some grace after their lengthy partnership.

'In that case, my offer is reduced to a half.'

'That's how it will be then,' the showman snapped. 'Call in again. The beast won't last till spring.' But the grey man said he was leaving soon, and his client might not wait that long.

Next morning, on seeing how close to death the creature was the showman thought – what difference would it make if he were to remove the horn now? It could be dead by Thursday. He sought the stranger and found him packing his bags. 'I've reconsidered,' he told him. 'You can have the horn if you wait till tonight.' Then he demanded half the fee in advance.

After a poor day's business, when people asked for their

money back and others quarrelled as the animal did nothing
but lie in a corner, the showman put up the shutters for the
last time.

He had a selection of blades from a poor surgeon who hired
equipment out to desperate people. It might have been an
unpleasant business sawing the horn with the animal dead, but
like this, still alive and weak, it made him feel disloyal.

Like cutting toenails – he tried to convince himself. But the
rhinoceros slumped and turned away. He had expected it to be
more difficult, expected it to kick and snap. He had padded
himself with bolsters to protect his bones, and looked strangely
swollen as he knelt before the beast.

The horn felt soft, like cutting through soap. He'd thought it
would be harder, like sawing through a tooth or solid bone, but
the horn came away cleanly, hollow and grey with a smooth
edge at the base. He held it in his hand and sat back on his
heels. The animal gleamed with sickly radiance in the half light:
he thought then how its eggy eyes were disturbingly human.

With the horn in a pouch he walked slowly to the rendezvous,
mulling over how he would invest his money, how his business
skills would prove invaluable for the life he was planning. Already
he had decided to ignore the original agreement and press for a
better deal.

'Look at my bruises,' he said showing the stranger old marks
from a brawl he had crossed one night. 'It put up a fight. I
could have died alone in that place. I took a chance for you
. . .' He limped towards a bench. The stranger set the money
on the wooden table-top. 'Then at least the surgeon's fee,' the
showman said, when he saw he would not budge, 'for scraping
the horn clean of fatty matter and . . . blood.'

The stranger counted twenty ducats more. 'For your lies,'
he said, letting the coins drop through his fingers. His eyes
narrowed to two grey slits. 'And for your disloyalty – ' he
fingered the horn as he spoke – 'You will pay a price.'

'Drinks all round!' the showman bellowed, ignoring the other
who, clutching his acquisition, slipped away and was swallowed
by a fog rising from the canals.

*

When the showman woke next morning he felt uncommonly sore with a terrible headache. He couldn't feel his hands, as he fumbled for and failed to find his pipe. He didn't recognise anything. He must have ended up in a bordello, one new to him, there was the familiar smell, but stronger. Christ, someone ought to wash. He couldn't remember the woman, he just hoped he hadn't fallen in with one of the elderly Magdalenes from the square. He would go as soon as he found his trousers.

It was impossible to focus properly. He saw a series of flat shadows moving in front of his eyes. He felt dazed like the time he'd been set upon by students, when his skull had been well and truly cracked, and his good topcoat stolen, right off his back.

Something rustled. He felt a sharp spike in his arse. He was laying on straw. What sort of a place had he come to? A pain across his forehead was tightening by the minute. He must have drunk the place dry.

He felt a sharp kick, and turning his head saw, some feet away, a pair of calf boots which he recognised as his own. He'd been robbed and now the thief had returned to kick him wearing his own boots! He'd know them anywhere. He'd had them made specially from kid-skin, the finest, blondest hides. He shouted thief, but there was no sound. His tongue was swollen in his mouth. It felt as if it would choke him. Then he heard laughter overhead but when he looked, shadows on the edge of his vision fluttered away.

At first he could only make out edges. Everything looked flat as if the world was cut from paper. He recognised a noise: that high human sound of laughter. Surrounded by edges, he distinguished the grey man who'd bought the horn from him. He was laughing, and that might have been strange enough, but even stranger was the man who partnered him. A huge man who looked horribly familiar. And a dull memory told him that once he had been such a man himself. It was like seeing a reflection. Bigger than he'd imagined, uglier too. And he had never been vain, only about his legs. Fine legs, well muscled. These were over muscled, and the impudent lout was now wearing his boots! Was this what the grey man had meant when he said he would pay for his disloyalty? Had he returned with an accomplice to steal back the payment?

Slowly, he tried to get up. He put a hand out to steady himself and saw instead of fingers a split and calloused hoof, a useless thing. He sweated to raise himself on all fours. The effort of lifting his heavy neck exhausted him. He trembled with animal fear, watching the bestial showman who was flexing his fingers, moving his thumbs experimentally. Carnevale had worked its magic. The grey man was watching both of them as if this was some experiment when for the first time man and beast might see each other, and recognise the horror of their natures. This was the savage morning after the endless party. The Carnevale drum beat stopped. In the silence the grey stranger laughed. Then everyone joined in. The stranger laughed, like everyone else, without a trace of compassion.

TRUE ROMANCE

Caroline Forbes

Caroline Forbes was born in London. *The Needle on Full*, a collection of science fiction short stories was published in 1985. In 1992, her first radio play *Michelle and the Landlady* received an award in the *Radio Times* Comedy and Drama Awards. After living in Lancashire and Australia she has now settled in Norfolk.

TRUE ROMANCE was first broadcast on Radio 4, read by Siriol Jenkins.

TRUE ROMANCE

'You picked number three and that's our Stella from Lancaster,'
Cilla said; the screen went back and I thought, 'Oh no.' I wanted
to call the other girls back. He'd have got on a treat with
Margaret from Epping. She'd have a posh job in the city and
was all padded shoulders and Perrier water. The other one, Kim
from Dunstable, was quite nice even with the squeaky voice,
and honest to God she looked like a model. Still, it would teach
me to go on *Blind Date* and make a fool of myself.

Don't get me wrong. He was handsome enough. He had dark
curly hair and really lovely blue eyes, a bit like Lovejoy. The
audience certainly went for him, you could hear them whistling
and cheering when he first came on. My friend Pat was in the
fourth row and she put both her thumbs up so I knew she didn't
think he was a dishrag. But he just wasn't my type. I don't
really know what is. I think I prefer blonds, you know those
sort of insipid looking ones with pale skin and thin wrists. He
was called Gareth. I should have known when I heard that. But
when the cameras are on you, well you can't think of anything
else. I mean there are millions watching. Not that millions are
going to be watching now, are they? They'll scrub the whole
episode I expect.

He made me pick the card out. I was praying it wouldn't be
doing Outward Bound in the Lake District because I went last
year with our Stephen and never again. But of course it wasn't. It
was the trip to Amsterdam. Cilla read out the details: champagne
flight, trips round the city and a romantic cruise down the canals.
It sounded great and we promised we'd be back the next week
to tell her all about it.

The champagne flight was a bit of a washout. By the time
they'd got airborne and passed the glasses round we had to

139

belt up and land. I think the film crew got most of it. Tony and Len. I liked them. You could tell they were glad I hadn't picked the Lake District. But Gareth was a bit browned off with my choice of date. He'd have been happier driving JCBs round sand-dunes or jet-setting off to New York. He'd been to Amsterdam before, several times. He told me about it several times too. He kept going on about how he knew the Real Amsterdam and how the tourists had ruined it. He meant common people like me though he didn't say so. Still, I was determined to enjoy myself. I'd never been to Amsterdam before. It was an adventure.

Don't get me wrong. I've been abroad quite a few times, two holidays in the Algarve and a weekend jaunt to Paris with Brenda Hopkins. I like travelling. I like the way different places have different characters. Paris was, well, a bit snooty but quite charming if you ignored the bull. Portugal was more like a wide boy off the market, all hairy chest and flashing eyes. And where I live, Lancaster's a little old lady who can still cause a few heads to turn.

Mrs Baker who lives above the shop and does for the vicar said she thought Amsterdam was lovely. She went on one of those bulb field holidays. She said it was clean, which is key for Mrs Baker. So all in all I was really excited about coming and thought: never mind about Gareth. But it was hard right from the start.

They laid on a car to drive us from the airport and Gareth only went and talked to the driver in Dutch. It made me squirm. Don't get me wrong, I wish I could speak it like him. But you could tell he was just trying to impress and I was glad when the driver just stared at him as though he were daft. But I didn't really care. It was a lovely hot sunny day and I just looked out of the window and let it all roll over me. I knew Holland was flat, I'm not that ignorant. But in reality it seemed much flatter, like it had been ironed out, smoothed down by some giant hand. I'm not used to that absolute flatness with nothing to mark the edges. It was weird. The sky was a huge blue glass dome sitting on top, holding everything under pressure. Underneath, the surface was flattened by its weight. Houses, cars, fields and trees all seemed really little and squashed. I stuck my head out of the window and felt the pressure, the air filling my head with a kind of energy. I wanted to ask the driver to stop but I knew Gareth wouldn't let him. I tried to talk to Gareth about it but he started going on about polders and dykes and people per square inch. The driver smiled at me though. He was blond.

We checked into a hotel in Amsterdam and Tony and Len said they had to suss out locations so could we go for coffee and meet them for lunch. I wanted to say, take me with you. Anyways I think they wanted to be alone, if you get my drift. Gareth was moving into his stride now, remembering out loud all the other times he'd been to Amsterdam on business. He said he knew this nice little place and marched me off.

We sat outside a café on the Prinsengracht. I can say that quite well now. Prinsengracht. It was a lovely little place and I had hot chocolate and a cake. You could watch all the Dutch people walking by, they were dead casual which was amazing because Amsterdam was magic.

I was beginning to feel like I'd landed on another planet. And I'm afraid it made me a bit short with Gareth. He thought communicating meant telling me all the things he knew, and by God he knew a lot. It was like someone had pressed a button marked 'Amsterdam' in his head and all he could do was spout out information.

I wanted him to be quiet so much, because the truth was I was falling in love with Amsterdam. And you can't do that properly while some idiot is rattling on about per capita income and the twenty-three different types of cannabis he smoked on his last visit. The drive had emptied my head and now it was filling up with all those beautiful houses, tall and thin with pitched roofs and tiles and dead pretty decorations And the water everywhere, reflecting the buildings and the trees, making it all so romantic. I've never been in love before, not with a man anyway and though I did have a brief flirtation with a city when me and Brenda Hopkins walked round the old Boulogne city walls eating chocolate cornettos, it wasn't the real thing. But this was. No build-up, no foreplay, love at first sight.

I did try with Gareth, honest. I mean he picked me and I should have been more grateful. But the more I loved

Amsterdam the more I wanted him to bugger off. There's nothing wrong in knowing things, God I'm a librarian, I spend my day surrounded by facts. But he just wanted to spout it all out, how Amsterdam was built on logs, how the marshes were drained, what its history was, how much, how big, on and on. And he spoke really slowly like he was speaking to a small child. Except I caught him staring at my boobs a few times, so he'd noticed something.

It was a relief to go back to the hotel and meet up with Tony and Len. They'd cheered up a lot and we had quite a jolly lunch. Len told me about the market on Waterloo Plein and Tony said they were glad it was an overnight job because there were some great clubs to go to. Gareth didn't say much. I don't think he liked Tony and Len. I don't think they liked him.

After lunch we had to get on with the job. I mean there had to be a film and pictures to take back to Cilla. They took us off to a clog shop and we got dressed up as a little Dutch boy and girl. It was a laugh. I looked a right idiot in a big white hat and I didn't think Gareth would ever forgive them for making him wear huge baggy trousers and yellow clogs. Tony and Len dragged us round flower markets and diamond shops and art galleries till I was completely knackered. We ended up in another café overlooking the river Amstel watching the boats while they went off in a huddle to decide if they'd got enough shots. And all the time I was floaty and a bit faint because that's how love makes you feel. I was blushing like a kid, like it was written across my face in obvious embarrassing letters, Amsterdam I Love You.

Then there was dinner. The big romantic number on the canal boat. I was dreading it. I'd bought a new dress specially for the trip and borrowed Brenda Hopkins' silver dangly earrings. The dress was dead trendy, red and off the shoulder, but I nearly didn't wear it.

I sat in the hotel room staring at that silly oval face in the mirror and thought, what the heck are you doing girl? Going out to dinner with a complete nerd who'll bore you all through the meal and try and get into your knickers after. It was my fault for entering of course, though I blamed Mrs Baker. If she hadn't bet me £10, I'd be home now getting our Stephen's tea and waiting for Mum to get home from her shift. And it was silly to be in love with a city. A city's just a city, full of dirt and mean people. That's what the face in the mirror said back at me. But in the end I did get dressed up. And Tony and Len said I looked fantastic and Len said could he borrow the earrings sometime which made *me* laugh. He looked really cute, Len, in a little green bow-tie and a yellow jacket. He bought me a drink in the bar while we waited and told me funny stories about the last time they came to Amsterdam with this pair who had fancied the pants off each other and how he and Tony had had to pry them apart to keep the film decent. Gareth looked like a penguin.

It didn't matter. The evening was a dream. Floating down the canals with all the illuminations on the bridges shining and the black water dappled with light and colour. I drank too much wine but I didn't care. The air was so warm and soft and everywhere there were people wandering about, leaning over the bridges, cycling down the streets, talking and laughing.

There were people sat out on their houseboats drinking and smoking, their voices spiralling upwards, lifted by the night air. There were people high up, leaning out of windows calling down to friends on the pavements. I know lots of them were awful, like Dutch Gareths. I know lots of them probably cheated and lied and allsorts. But that night nothing mattered.

I could hear Gareth talking in the background but I wasn't with him any more, I was with the city. He did show a bit of interest when we went through the red light area, peering up through the window of the boat to try and see what was going on. There was one woman sitting in her underwear in a big glass window smoking a cigarette. Gareth saw her and laughed and I hated him. He was making fun of her but you could hear the edge of desire in his voice. Then he stared at me, and pressed his leg against mine under the table. I wanted to say, 'I didn't wear this dress for you. I wore it for Amsterdam.' He was just a bystander, sneering at everything and taking what he wanted. I mean that's no way to treat a city is it?

But in the end he took a bit too much. He must have been drunk, that's what they said. We got off the boat no problem and went to stand by the edge and watch the water while Tony and Len called a taxi.

He just fell in. I don't know how it happened. One minute he was standing beside me and I could feel his hand moving down my back and I was about to say, watch it sonny, and the next he was gone. The police said it was really bad luck. He must have hit his head on the way down.

They lay him on his side while we waited for an ambulance. His face was all white and surprised. It must have been the first time he actually came into contact with the city at all. Tony and Len went into overdrive on the pictures and on-the-spot interviews. You could see *News at Ten Special* written all over their faces. Everyone was really upset and there was a big enquiry by the TV people. But it wasn't anybody's fault. Not really.

Of course I couldn't go back on the show the next week. It was a shame because I could have done a good talk and Cilla's dead nice, just like you'd think she'd be.

STORMING THE BARRICADES

Jonathan Treitel

Jonathan Treitel was born in London. He worked as a physicist in California and has a doctorate in philosophy. His short stories have appeared in various magazines and regularly on Radio 3 and 4. He is also the author of two novels.

STORMING THE BARRICADES was first broadcast on Radio 3, read by Harry Towb.

STORMING THE BARRICADES

So I am going for my regular stroll before lunch along Ocean Drive. I can usually make it past seventeen palm trees – my cardiovascular specialist says I have the heart of a man of fifty, provided I stop and lean on my Zimmer frame when short of breaths. Then suddenly, there in front of me on the beach, silhouetted against the sheer blue of the Atlantic, is the most beautiful woman I have ever seen in my entire life. Long flowing hair, round eyes, endless legs, skinny, bony, and I don't understand why she doesn't do something about her eyebrows – but definitely a class act. I'm getting a side view of her buttercup yellow bathing costume. At last she turns. And I see she has the kind of expression which, when I was young, used to be described as sultry. She pouts.

So no wonder I don't notice the fool who is stumbling into me. He's a grown man, bald except for puffs of white hair on either side like his ears are smoking, and surely he's old enough to know better. Of course I blame him and he blames me. We call each other dangers to society and capitalist hyenas and shmocks and ask why we can't use the eyes in our heads . . . and he is yelling, 'Irv Tishbaum!' And I reach out and hug him as far as my Zimmer lets me: 'Harry Halle! I haven't seen you in sixty years! How come you're still alive? You haven't changed one bit!' And does he hug me back? Does he even smile? Does he ever!? He brandishes his walking stick, '*No pasaran!*' And I say: 'Don't give me that shit!' And now again we're waving our fists and screaming all the bad names in the book.

And there's a story behind all this that you have to know. Back in 1934, when Harry ran off to Spain to join the Abraham Lincoln Brigade, I promised to go too. But at the last moment . . . you understand how it was: I had obligations to my parents, to my aunt Edith and my uncle Joey, may they rest in peace. Also I suffered from flat feet. And there was the matter of Harry's girl, Essie Flieger . . .

So I am trying to explain to him about my longstanding podiatric problem, and that it turned out Essie was sweet on a boxer, Joe somebody – but Harry won't let me finish my sentence. He's shrieking, 'Shmat shmeet! Why couldn't you have died in Huesca like a hero! Why couldn't you have been buried in the rubble of Seville!' But he calms down, and he tells me he has an apartment in the renovated complex on Collins and 4th. I let him know about my suite in the Seashell Hotel on Ocean with a sea view. And we swap kvetches about cockroaches the size of rabbits, 'Rabbit nothing!' says Harry, 'My bugs are big as elephants!' – and I think Harry is on the point of agreeing with me about something.

But just then a young man wearing a Dolphins cap back to front asks if we could please haul our asses off the sidewalk since we're standing in shot. So of course we refuse. 'It's a free country,' Harry growls, and I interject, 'It ought to be.' Meanwhile a girl assistant is adjusting the model's hair. The Dolphins man asks us again, more politely. Harry hooks his stick on to my frame, and hums 'We Shall Overcome' and I try to remember the words . . . there's something in it about a tree and a sea – and finally we decide to husband our legitimate wrath for more important battles to come, and we head inland . . . The photographer makes his come-hither gesture. The model, rolling her head and torso and hips in an exaggerated motion, advances towards the camera very slowly as if a big wind was blowing right at her, or as if she was old.

So Harry and I, soon we're across on the other side of Ocean – I can still see the beach if I peer through the top half of my bifocals: the model is repeating her strut over and over – and we're hanging loose by the take-out window of the La Independencia diner. And I'm sipping a cortadito which comes in a little plastic cup, bitter and strong and delicious. Harry asks if I still have any illusions about the hegemony of the Brazilian agribusiness-military complex, and it's not impossible the fashion-photographer on the beach is in the pay of the FBI.

148

He has the perfect cover. And meanwhile Harry is munching on a guava cake which is a boon for his gastric juices, and whaddya know only last February in the lobby of a Woody Allen film he runs into little Harriet Zemansky with the stick out ears and the dirty jokes, who used to make us all laugh so much at meetings of the Central Brooklyn Young Socialist League. She's in fine shape apart from her hearing isn't so great and living in the Frick Residence on 15th. So Harry gives me his own phone number, and hers. And I give him mine, and Fred Minsky's and Leo Cowan's and I say that Leo probably knows where Ray Fisch is hiding out, somewhere downtown, on the far side of the MacArthur Causeway – yes, famous Ray who went underground for twenty years. And Fred told me Lenny and Minnie Brown have relocated down here, though of course I haven't spoken to the Browns since the Molotov-Ribbentrop pact. Also there was somebody else supposed to have come south but I can't remember the name just like that . . . And Harry wonders out loud what ever happened to Essie, our very own La Passionaria of the CBYSL. I shrug. He says she sent him a courageous, inspiring New Year card in '35 but he lost it in a fortified position somewhere south of Catalonia. He shows me the scar on his shin where they cut out the shrapnel. Sweat is dripping from our brows. Iced water comes gratis in disposable paper cones. Meanwhile a radio is on inside, playing that Cuban music, and the girl who works there, a slim dark one, is rumbaing on her own. I tell Harry she is the most beautiful woman I have ever seen in my entire life. And he actually agrees! The trash is full, so we drop the paper cones on the sidewalk where they lie among other used cones.

You know how it is. First you meet one person from the old days, then suddenly you're running into another and another. It never rains but it pours. Simone Moskowitz in Flamingo Park . . . her nurse is very helpful, but we can't make poor Simone understand who I am. And just a few weeks later, on the trunk of the huge tree outside the A & P somebody had plastered a flier: 'Air Conditioned Temple Beth Raphael Proudly Presents The World Famous Cantor Acclaimed Throughout America And

Europe As An Eminent Successor To The Immortal Cantorial Giants Of The Past Golden Era . . .' and you'll never guess who just rolled up in his battery powered wheelchair and is scrawling over the poster OPIUM OF THE PEOPLE in red? Marty Silber! So I say: well I never. And he tells me I'm a lily-livered poltroon to break with the Party in '39 but he's prepared to let bygones be bygones. He raises his clenched fist in the Popular Front salute. And we get chatting. He's just taken a lease on a brand new condo by Lummus Park – and guess who's got a condo in the same building? It's Doris 'Free Love' Kaye! I give him my special wink. And he tells me Doris is a new woman since they put in her pacemaker.

A golden opportunity to bring together the old gang! In fact I intend to arrange a get-together that winter, but what with one thing and another – you know how it is (my heart man said I should take things easy for a while). I put it off and I put it off and already it's summer again – which isn't a good time for getting anything accomplished (I know it's always summer here, but summer is *summer*). But no more delays! We're none of us getting any younger. I reserve a functions room in my hotel, and pay the deposit up front. I phone around. I even post a notice in the window of La Independencia and Danny's Genuine New York Deli: 'The Reunion Of The CBYSL Will Take Place At 6 PM On August 22nd In The Panorama Room Of The Seashell Hotel.' No need to explain what the initials stand for – those who know, know.

'Irv!' 'Marty!' 'Susie!' 'Bob!' 'Lionel!' 'Ray!' 'Stanley!' 'Doris!' 'Harry!' 'Simone!' 'Fred!' 'Leo!' 'Power to the People!' 'Long time no see!' 'You don't look a day older!' 'Second Front, Now!' Everyone in there shouting and gladhanding, drinking selzer and Budweiser (except that Fred is organising a faction to boycott the brewing companies) and passing the peanuts. Everyone complaining about the terrible humid weather and the phoniness of this year's Presidential election and their medical conditions. I balance in the centre of the room on my Zimmer, greeting the guests as they appear out of the elevator. 'Once a CBYSL-er, always a CBYSL-er!' I cry – waving them over in the direction of the no-host bar. Ray is trying to persuade the bartender to break his shackles and join a party if not the Party. The air conditioner is buzzing like a trapped wasp. The room is way up at the top of the hotel. The huge picture window gives a glorious view of the beach and the ocean but not as glorious as all that: big black storm clouds on the horizon, and a wind is attacking the fronds of the palm trees.

Suddenly the clouds are overhead and we are in the midst of a downpour. The window is splattered with an almost opaque screen of rain, and the noise of it on the roof is so great we have to shout. 'Remember when they fired the water cannon at us when we fought the scabs in Jersey City in '38!' Stanley yells. And maybe we don't remember – you can't trust Stanley: he was CP all the way through '56 – but what the hell, it might be true. Harriet asks what's going on, and Ray screeches an explanation in her hearing aid. Simone starts whimpering, and her nurse feeds her some chicken soup from a vacuum flask. The latecomers arrive soaked to the bone. 'Jerry!' 'Gloria!' 'Morris!' 'Lenny and Minnie!' 'Harriet!' 'Marty!' Marty is tossing his head throwing water off his mop of white hair the way a dog shakes its body. 'I got lost,' he accuses me, 'somewhere in your crummy atrium!' I tell him: 'It's not crummy, it's Art Deco.' 'I'm old enough to remember when we didn't say Art Deco. We said shyster builders with mob connections hiding lousy construction under a dollop of pink stucco!' And Marty swivels his wheelchair round so as to sneak up on Gloria's behind and give it a little tweak, and she, furious, denounces him for swallowing the cover-up on the Kamenev-Zinoview show trials hook, line and sinker . . . Well, you can't leave Harry out of a good argument! He's charging into the thick of it, thwacking the fitted carpet with his stick, discovering a grievous lack of dialectical comprehension on both sides. And I inform Harry I am in agreement with him one hundred per cent. He flashes me a scowl.

Then, just as suddenly as it started, the rain stops. A fierce gale instead. The wind howls and whines. Clouds go speeding by like in a time-lapse film. Lightning upon lightning; thunder. The elevator doors open, and who comes out, perfectly dry, protected by a scarlet umbrella . . .

'Essie!' Harry and I are shouting. I manoeuvre towards her on my frame, but he gets in first with his stick. She furls her umbrella, and offers her wry smile to everyone. I guess her hair is dyed and maybe her teeth aren't her own, but she is still the most beautiful woman in the whole world. 'How did you hear about this?' I ask. Harry butts in, 'How long you been living here?' She shakes us both by the hand. She tells us she lives in Brooklyn, in the old neighbourhood. She's here on vacation, visiting her niece . . . and she saw the notice in the New York Deli.

Harry mumbles at her: 'Remember when I went off to Spain with the Abe Lincoln, and you said you could no longer be my girl because I refused to accept the legitimacy of the role played by POUM in the Popular Front struggle . . .' I get in my piece: 'Remember when you left me for Joe, just after you and I had the big fight over Bakunin's critique of Marx . . .'

Essie gives us both a sidelong glance. She opens her purse and passes around photos of her grandchildren.

The gale is getting stronger. The picture window itself thrums. The roof creaks. Outside, a gull is shot past like a bullet. I could swear an orange lifevest goes flying by. The palm trees are dancing – no, drowning.

It's a while till we hear the phone ring. Marty picks it up; listens a minute; slams it down. It rings again. I take the call. The voice of some capitalist lackey – frightened the way they always are. 'This is the manager. You're going to have to leave. All of you! Now! While the elevator is still operational!' I turn to the CBYSL: 'There's a man here says we should all come down. And what is the people's answer?' Essie presses the down button on the elevator. Harry booms, 'No!' 'No!' We comrades echo, stamp our feet and bang our Zimmers and slam our glasses on the bar. The telephone voice says, 'Unless you leave at once, the police –' Ray seizes the phone from me and hurls it against the wall.

The storm doesn't let up. The hotel sways. The electricity gives out. Then the place is dim and the air is stuffy and the elevator buttons have stopped glowing. And all of us (except Essie who has seated herself in an armchair and is busy reducing

152

her nose shine with the aid of a powder compact) are heaving the drinks table in front of the elevator to make a kind of barricade, and piling chairs on top of it, and balancing the trash can on the chairs as a kind of booby trap . . .

Just as we are finishing this, Mr Hernandez the manager, followed by a cop, fools us all by coming in through the fire exit. They are panting. The cop is scratching his head. Mr Hernandez is saying to no one in particular, 'It's not safe. Especially at your time of life.' The cop shows the manager a photograph of me and Harry plus a young woman in the background wearing a buttercup yellow bathing costume: 'Those are the ringleaders.'

At last we are in the eye of the storm. The sky clears to a brilliant blue, and chunks of masonry and a shoe and a paperback book and a surfboard go whizzing past. The ceiling groans. It makes a rattling noise. And we are all (except Essie) – even Simone's nurse, even Leroy the bartender – linking arms and forming a line in front of the barricade. I'm supported on either side, so I'm free of my Zimmer. Marty has been pulled out of his wheelchair. Simone is lifted by her nurse. *Essie,* I implore, but just in my head, *our only Essie, the Essie we have dreamed of through all these tough years. Beautiful, fervent, ideologically pure Essie, what has happened to you, where are you now when we need you most?* Also Harry is staring at her hungrily as she puts her cosmetics case back in her purse and pats her mouth with a kleenex to remove excess lipstick. He's thinking the same thoughts – and all the other CBYSL-ers are focusing their gazes and their desires on her – and at last she rises from the armchair and comes over and rests her arms around mine and Harry's shoulder. Her head is tilted back like a heroine in a Socialist Realist poster. And it's she who begins our song, the good old song, the Internationale. Most of us remember at least half of the words. Harry sings along in Catalan, Ray (always Mister Show-off) does it in the original French. Lenny and Minnie know the Hebrew version. Miraculously even Simone sings along in Yiddish. 'Arise, ye damned of the earth . . . there shall be no more rulers and ruled . . . let us make a clean sweep of the past . . .' And with a mighty crackling whoosh the roof lifts free and skims away, and there is nothing but sky overhead.

LIVING HISTORY

Martyn Read

Martyn Read has twice won the Giles Cooper Award for his radio plays. *Scouting for Boys* and *Waving to a Train* – the latter was subsequently made into a television film. He has written fifteen plays for radio, and has been an actor for more than twenty years. He lives in Henley-on-Thames.

LIVING HISTORY was broadcast on Radio 4, read by John Moffatt.

LIVING HISTORY

When the Reverend William Bendigo was born, the great and glorious reign of Queen Victoria had still eight years to run. Baden-Powell had not yet held out at Mafeking. Kitchen-maids still bobbed and said 'Yes, 'm.' And the combustion engine was still a spluttering infant – so that all that circled the sky above the churchyard were the timeless rooks. Houses were lit by oil-lamp – as is still the Reverend Bendigo's bedroom, where I now sit. It is unusual to find me here on a Saturday. For forty years my regular visits have been on Wednesday morning, when we play a game of draughts, and Sunday afternoon, when I read to him from the Prayer Book.

I sit quietly by the big brass bed and watch the old man breathing gently. The thin, oval face is stretched with translucent skin, delicate like a woman's. Two bright red spots mark his cheeks. His fine white hair is neatly parted. No doubt he has been recently scrubbed by that old bitch of a housekeeper in the kitchen. On his nose, a pair of ancient gold-rimmed spectacles.

I glance through the window to the little church where my friend was incumbent for exactly fifty years, and watch the rooks wheel lazily. The clock shows a little before half past eleven. My eyes wander lovingly over the familiar old room, unaltered for a century. And I notice that a decanter and two glasses have been set upon the bedside cabinet. I smile at old William's sense of occasion – an occasion he evidently wishes me to share. For today, at noon precisely, the Reverend Bendigo will be one hundred years old. More remarkably, he was born in this very house, in this very room, in this very bed! And sadly, but understandably, he has decided, again on the stroke of noon, to close the account. I would not wish him to be alone.

157

I like the past. To me it is more real than the present, and certainly more comfortable. The future I never contemplate, which is strange, given my calling as an undertaker. I eat simply, drink moderately, and dress plainly. For recreation, I collect old Last Wills and Testaments – and the remembrances of my friend's rich life. But I confess that this next half-hour, this near future, disturbs me. I do not mean the petty griefs of death – I know from observation such things pass soon enough. No, I fear the closing door. I fear the silence of my lexicon, my archive – my living history. The church clock strikes the half. Mr Bendigo does not stir. The harridan downstairs was more than usually unpleasant this morning. 'Vulture' she called me. 'Coming here and picking the bones of the poor old man's memory.' I have long since ceased trying to explain the mutual benefits of my visits. Vulture, indeed. I stare out of the window and watch the rooks.

It is true I have taped several hours of conversation with Mr Bendigo (I have the recording machine in my pocket now). I have a dozen notebooks. I know his austere parson father. I have seen the minutiae of a Victorian village. The harvest suppers, the Christmas Waits – the coming of mains water. I have shared the national shock when the old bombazine matriach of Osborne unbelievably died. I have watched W.G.Grace stroke a ball to the boundary. Journeyed to the trenches and seen the dug-out he shared with Wilfred Owen. Indeed, he has recited to me a slightly improper limerick which the great poet composed. But my most treasured morsel is this: he has taken me to a golden garden party where a pot-bellied, cigar-ashed man stared down at my young friend. 'Odd name, Bendigo,' said His Majesty King Edward the Seventh. This to me is thrilling, the jewel of my collection thus far. And yet I sense there is a greater morsel he has to give; one final ruby parcelled up in dust and time – and my thoughts shift at once to the old widow of Windsor. Was there Majesty in her movement? Splendour in her speech? I put it from my mind, not daring to hope.

'You have come on a Saturday, Geoffrey.' The silky voice

starts me from my reverie. I turn and see the familiar half-smile. 'This is unprecedented.'

'I have come to wish you a very happy one hundredth birthday, Mr Bendigo.' I say. 'Shall we play a game of draughts?'

'No, no more draughts, Geoffrey,' he replies. 'I have known for some time you allow me to win.' The pale eyes mock my discomfort.

'My name is Ronald, Mr Bendigo.'

Geoffrey was his only son, whose Spitfire was shot down in 1943. It is the only lapse in an otherwise remarkable memory. At least, I trust it is the only lapse.

'Then shall I ask Mrs Handscombe to fetch you some tea?' I enquire, eyeing the decanter.

'I'm sure you would prefer to broach a little Madeira,' he smiles, 'in honour of so indelible a day.'

I reach for the wine. 'Before you taste,' says Mr Bendigo, 'you will, of course, wish to learn its provenance. This is the last of a case presented by Mr Nehru to Earl Mountbatten, a distant connexion of mine, at the time of partition in 1947. You may pour.'

'Such a provenance can only enhance its taste.' I cry, handing him a glass. 'Your health, sir.'

Nectar! I glance at the clock and decide to bring the subject round to Wills.

'You will be interested to know, Mr Bendigo, that yesterday I added to my little collection. The last wishes of a wartime draper written in Esperanto.'

'Esperanto!' chuckles my friend. 'I remember the fad. And can you decipher it?'

'Some of the words are nearly familiar,' I reply, 'but the whole appears to mean nothing at all.'

Mr Bendigo looks lazily into my eyes. 'Similarly,' he says, 'a great number of facts, in themselves interesting, may add up to something equally meaningless.'

I stare at him. 'I do not follow you, Mr Bendigo,' I falter. The church clock strikes the three-quarters.

'Now, we do not have much time,' says the centenarian briskly, 'and I wish you to know how I have arranged matters.'

I manage to shelve Mr Bendigo's puzzling remark. I can always concentrate on a Will. His savings, I think, must be substantial.

'My savings I have left to an ex-Servicemen's Charity.' I nod at the properness of this. There is yet the house, purchased from the Church many years ago. To live among such tremendous ghosts!

'The house, of course, will go to Mrs Handscombe. I believe she has plans.'

Indeed she has. By the end of the summer it will be the Rectory Bed-and-Breakfast, with hot and cold running.

'Finally,' says Mr Bendigo, 'I have given a great deal of thought to my Collection.'

Ah, the Collection. Piles of unread documents. Albums of sepia photographs. A stuffed kingfisher in a bell jar. I modestly lower my eyes.

'I have decided to bequeath my collection to the County Museum.'

I sip my wine but taste nothing.

'But as a tangible token of the many, *many* hours we have spent together – er, Ronald, I should like you to have my set of draughts.'

I nod dumbly. I hear the rooks and remember the approaching hour. I grasp at a straw.

'Sir,' I say wildly, 'would you like me to read from the Prayer Book?'

'No I damn well would not!' he cries. I must be febrile. I think I heard Mr Bendigo swear.

'But think, sir! You are about to meet the greatest ghost of all!'

'Am I?' he says. 'I might just as easily return in a week's time as an otter.'

Bewildered, I consider the idea of Mr Bendigo living in a hole by the river and diving for fish.

'You are angry that after so many years of devotion, you come away empty-handed.'

'On the contrary,' I reply. 'I enjoy draughts. I am never short of trade and my rooms are adequate.'

'Personally,' says Mr Bendigo, 'I could never be comfortable living over the shop, as you do. Not a night passing without a cadaver or two below.'

Cadaver, I muse.

'And you have filled my present with your rich past,' I continue. 'That is bequest enough.'

'The past is merely an adjunct to the present. It cannot replace it. It is arid. Sterile.' He sighs wearily. 'I have been remiss, Gerald.'

I am becoming confused as to my nomenclature.

'I look at the man and see only the Brylcreemed choirboy who always sang in tune and never threw hymn-books about. I have been guilty of feeding your pleasure and not your soul. Tit-bits to a magpie. Any pretty thing.'

A magpie picking a cadaver. His watery eyes hold mine.

'Even today I daresay you've come sniffing for one final scrap. But you've picked me clean.'

A cadaver with skin-stretched bones.

'Mr Bendigo,' I whisper, 'your past is not arid. It is rich, sustaining. It is my life!'

He looks out of the window to the clock.

'Suppose,' he murmurs, 'that all I have told you, all that you have gleaned over the years – suppose, now, that none of it is true.'

'Not true?' I croak.

'Suppose it is all a fiction to feed you. What, then, would happen? To you?'

I teeter on the edge of a black abyss and am prevented from falling only by reaching for the decanter and pouring another glass of Nehru's best.

'I'll tell you what would happen,' says Mr Bendigo. 'You'd disappear. Gone. Nothing there.'

'Not true?' I repeat.

'You are too used to embracing death, Reginald. I bequeath you this: go out and grab life by the scruff of the neck. Throw hymn-books about.'

I have a brief vision of a fifty-year-old undertaker hopping about in a discoteque. The clock shows three minutes to noon. I begin to panic.

'Mr Bendigo!' I plead. 'What care I for cash and old rectories – only tell me that I have not built my house on sand.'

'Does it matter?'

'But you cannot mean me to believe that there was no Dr Grace; no King Edward; that Owen was not the author of that filthy limerick; that – that mains water did not arrive on the Fourth of May Nineteen Twenty One?'

'If you're so interested in plumbing,' he cries, 'you could have discovered that in the Municipal Records Office.'

Precious seconds tick by. I stare at the soon-to-be cadaver.

'There are only moments in which to compose myself,' says Mr Bendigo. 'You are used to embalming useless things. You will see that these old bones depart with dignity.' You can be assured of that, Mr Bendigo. Assured.

'But, sir, are you not afraid of going so ungraciously?'

'Oh, I would not wish to be ungracious.' A slow smile spreads across his face. 'They say every pleasure reserves its highest delight till its end. So. I *shall* tell you something.'

A surge of joy courses through me. Trembling, I lean forward to catch the failing voice, surreptitiously removing the recording machine from my pocket.

'Something which will perhaps be a crown for your collection – and which, beyond peradventure, *is* true.'

The clock begins to strike the quarters. I put my ear to the thin lips and close my eyes.

'What is it, Mr Bendigo, what is it?'

'On this my death-bed, Humphrey, I swear to you that as a very small boy . . .'

My heart pounds. 'Yes, Mr Bendigo, yes?'

'That as a small boy I did once meet . . .'

Pomp and majesty fill my mind's eye! Osborne, Windsor, Sandringham, Balmoral flash before me. The quarters conclude. A hanging silence.

'Speak, Mr Bendigo, speak! That once you did meet – ?'

The clock strikes the first hour. I sense a small exhalation in my ear.

'Mr Bendigo, please!' I open my eyes. 'Mr Bendigo?'

And I see his pale eyes glassy; the mocking smile frozen.

I switch off the machine, sit back and stare at my newest cadaver.

'Your bones shall indeed be accorded the utmost dignity, old friend,' I say as I reach into my pocket. I always carry with me two old pennies: one of King Edward, the other, of course, Victoria. I gently remove the pillow and lay the old head flat. 'The utmost dignity,' I repeat as I close the lids with my thumb. The door clicks open and the doyenne of Bed-and-Breakfast clumps in.

'He's gone then. We'll have a nice bit of mahogany and brass 'andles.' She hands me my scarf and bowler hat. 'You'll be pleased to leave my house now.'

I watch aghast as she unstops the decanter and takes a deep draught. 'Mrs Handscombe, please! That is a noble wine. A relic of the Raj.'

'Like 'ell,' says she. 'It's cooking sherry. I got it from the corner shop yesterday.'

I turn and look at Mr Bendigo.

'You'll be making arrangements, then?' says Mrs Handscombe. The two crowned heads balanced on the eyelids wink up at me.

'Oh yes,' I say. 'I shall be making arrangements.'

The funeral is simple and efficient, the mourners few. One or two old villagers and a veiled housekeeper pressing a handkerchief to her mouth as convincingly as an actress in the silent pictures. I shovel the first symbolic spadeful into the grave and watch the earth spatter onto the coffin I alone screwed down the night before. We disperse, and the rooks croak in the tree-tops.

And now I sit to one side of the spluttering gas-fire in my little sitting-room above the parlour. I sip a glass of the best Madeira I could buy and turn to the draughts board on the table by my chair. I consider the state of play, then leap-frog my black piece over five of white's. 'My game!' I say with quiet triumph. A gentle voice fills the room with some reminiscence of the Spanish Influenza epidemic of 1918. I press a button and the voice ceases. I refill my glass – and a second that stands on the table.

'Yes, most interesting,' I say. 'But I believe you were about to give me a very choice morsel? Something beyond peradventure true?'

I look enquiringly at the opposite chair. Mr Bendigo sits with his hands in his lap, the familiar half-smile embalmed on his bespectacled face. The picture of dignity. I wait respectfully for a few moments.

'No matter. I am sure it will come back to you. One day.'

I press the button again and sit back in my chair.

'Please continue,' I say, smiling at my old friend.

I have always been fascinated by living history.

RUN AND ASK DADDY
IF HE HAS ANY MORE MONEY

Fay Weldon

Fay Weldon is the author of numerous novels, stories and plays for television and radio. Her latest book is *Life Force*; she has a new novel published this spring.

RUN AND ASK DADDY IF HE HAS ANY MORE MONEY, was broadcast on Radio 4 and published in the *Radio Times*. The reader was Jane Lapotaire.

driving licence, should the passage of time not wipe out past misdeeds?

Daddy was the man Bettina referred to: he was at the back of the shop where the inexpensive trinkets were. Bettina was looking peculiarly attractive in a cashmere dress, in seasonal yellow, belted by a linked chain which for all anyone could tell was made of pure gold; the whole setting off her bosomy figure, little waist and black hair to advantage. Daddy was grey-suited, good-looking, gentlemanly and wore a solid gold tie-pin. David thought he looked extremely boring and rather stupid, but David would, wouldn't he?

'David, this has to stop,' Bettina had said to him in the History Tutorial Room one day, seven years ago. 'You are a married man and I'm going to be married too. The ceremony is next week. I wanted to tell you earlier but didn't like to, because I didn't want to upset you. You are the only man I'll ever really love but I have to think of my future. We have to be realistic. You could never support two homes in any comfort and I'm just not cut out for employment. I'm not that kind of person.' He'd thought his heart would break. He was surprised it went on beating. Later he'd told himself he was lucky to be out of a trivial, passing affair with such an unfeeling, whimsical person, but he'd never really believed himself. The truth was that he'd taken no real pleasure since in Milly's straight hair and earnest face. He could see Milly was good, but what a man wanted was something more than honest worth. Sometimes he felt guilty because others called his wife Frilly Mood, ironically, but then he'd tell himself she'd always been like that. Not his doing.

His blood ran cold – I say this advisedly. When David heard Bettina's voice – last heard on the floor behind the sofa in the History Tutorial Room – echoing through the shop at two minutes past four, he felt a chill strike down his head to his right shoulder, into his arm and down to his fingers, and he had the feeling that if that section of blood didn't warm up before it got back up to his heart, that organ would freeze and this time stop once and for all. So much a heart can stand, no more.

David turned his back on his customers, lest he be seen and

recognised by Bettina, and busied himself looking for a Peruvian crucifixion scene, grateful that his heart had survived the shock. But not before he had seen the little girl obediently leave her mother's side and head through shopping bags and spring-clad elbows towards her father. Bettina, near the door, was clearly interested in purchasing the papier-mâché bowl at £65; Daddy flicked through Easter cards at the back of the shop.

The Peruvian crucifixion scene consisted of six pieces in brightly glittering tin – a crimson Judas, a gold Jesus, a navy Pontius Pilate, a scarlet Mary Magdalene, a pale blue Madonna, and a black cross.

The little girl had red hair like David's own. Bettina had black hair; Daddy's was fair and painfully sparse, as if responsibility had dragged a lot of it out. The little girl must be six years old. Her front teeth were missing, to prove it.

The Easter cards were the cheapest things sold in the shop. For 75p you could buy cards depicting bunnies and chickens; from there on up to £2 you could find anything an artist in a time of recession could invent. Milly and David Frood saw the innovation of the Easter Card as one of the more sinister accomplishments of the Greetings Card Industry. Who ever in their youth had heard of an Easter card? All part of the commercialisation of religion, etc, etc. Obliged to live by commerce, the Froods despised commerce. Who doesn't?

Such things pass quickly through the mind when sights are seared into a man's heart, and he doesn't know what to think or feel, and he's gazing at a shelf.

David felt a familiar hand upon his arm. It was his wife's. 'Perhaps we should have another baby,' she said, to his further astonishment.

'Why now?' he asked. 'Why mention it now in the middle of such a rush?'

'Because we're always in a rush,' said Milly Frood, answering back, quite out of character, 'as anyone not on the dole these days is. And I just saw a little girl in the shop with hair the same lovely colour yours was when you were young: and I thought, last chance for a baby. I'm nearly forty now.' Before David could reply, a voice behind him said, 'Is there no one serving here?'

and Milly Frood turned quickly back to her work and David was let off the hook.

The familiar hand had cooked his food, burped his babies, returned the VAT, encouraged him in love and in illness, and it was a whole seven years since he had even been grateful for it, he realised. Now suddenly he was. But the habit of disparagement remained. 'Why mention it now?' he'd said, discouraging spontaneity, being disagreeable. He was ashamed of himself.

Another baby. David had not really wanted children in the first place: he had not wanted to get married. He would tell me about it when he lamented the everyday ordinariness of his life. The college, the kids, the shops, the bills, and never anything happening. But a man's seed bursts from him here and there, unwittingly, and a good man settles down to his responsibility, sometimes with a good heart, sometimes not. Another baby? David felt all of a sudden Milly could have anything she wanted. Suppose Bettina saw him; recognised him, greeted him? Then everything could simply fall apart. Supposing Daddy looked from his child's hair to the red beard, and remembered some clue, some time, some place? It's a wise man doubts his child's paternity, if his wife is Bettina. Supposing this, supposing that?

Let off the hook – but of course he wasn't let off the hook. The past may be another country, but there are frequently international flights from there to here, especially over the public holidays, when everyone leaves their homes and mills about in search of objects, not caring who remembers what. A papier-mâché bowl here, an Easter card there.

'Daddy,' said the little piping voice: was it like Sherry's? Was it like Baf's? It was. 'Mummy says do you have any more money?' Silence fell upon the shop. All waited for the reply: mothers, divorcées, widows, working women, and their escorts, should they have them. It's mostly women who shop. Slips of girls. Red-headed six-year olds with gap teeth looking trustingly up at alleged fathers. An honest question, honestly asked, in time of recession.

David turned: you cannot look at a single shelf for ever.

David caught Bettina's eye. Bettina smiled, in recognition, acknowledgement. Bettina's mouth was not quite as plump and full as once it had been. Everyone waited. A question publicly asked will be publicly answered. 'Tell your mother,' said Daddy loudly, 'the answer is no. My money's all gone and your mother has spent it.'

Daddy tipped over the box of Easter cards onto the floor and, parting customers with grey-suited elbows and gold-ringed hands, made his way to the door and out of it. The little girl ran weeping after him. David saw Daddy take his little girl's hand as they passed the window: he saw her smile: evidently the little girl cried easily and cheered up easily. Sherry had been like that.

If a woman has no money left, perhaps she'll turn back to love? Bettina stood irresolute for a moment, all eyes upon her. She looked at Milly, she looked at David. Then she said to Milly, 'I just love the shop,' and followed her husband and daughter out. It was four minutes past four.

Bettina had found herself pregnant: perhaps by one, perhaps by another. Perhaps she had not been unfeeling, whimsical in dismissing him, David, after all, behind the sofa in the History Tutorial Room. Perhaps the dismissal had been an act of love, to let the erring husband off the hook? Perhaps she had simply done what was right? In thinking better of Bettina, in forgiving her, David felt himself become quite free of her. And high time too. Seven whole years!

I just love the shop.

'What a nice woman,' said Milly. 'Saying that. Did she know you or something?'

'No, she didn't,' said David. 'And you're the nicest woman I know,' and he found that, though the first was a lie, the second was true. Happy Easter, everyone! Which speaks for itself: no need for explanation or excuse.

TRUMPET OF VICTORY

Carl Tighe

Carl Tighe was born in Handsworth, Birmingham. He is the author of two radio plays and several stage plays: in 1987 *A Whisper in the Wind* was winner of the All London Drama Prize. His first book was *Gdansk: National Identity in the Polish-German Borderlands* (Pluto, 1990), and his first collection of fiction was *Rejoice! and Other Stories* (Cape, 1992). He is currently working on a new collection of short stories, and now lives in Manchester.

TRUMPET OF VICTORY was first broadcast on Radio 4, and read by Stephen Moore.

TRUMPET OF VICTORY

A gentle but insistent tapping at the door of the apartment woke Jan. Still in long underwear, he groped his way down the hall and opened the door. It was Piotr.

'Is it safe to come in?'

'Sure, my wife is still asleep.'

They went back to the warmth of the kitchen. Jan put water on to boil and then resumed his sour milk. Piotr said:

'I've got some good news. Your trumpet's arrived.'

'Bloody liar.'

'Honest.'

'How d'you know?'

'My Milena shares a room with one of the assistants from the music shop. She said: "Tell your friend his instrument has come." But we have to collect it early. They're expecting a big delivery of Country and Western records today so we have to be there before the queue forms. If you pull yourself together you might even have time for a bit of a practice before the Great Moment.'

'The Great . . . ? Oh my God! I'd forgotten. It's today.'

'It's a great moment in the history of our country.'

'I don't feel like playing the trumpet. Great Moment or not.'

'You get dressed. I'll make coffee.'

Jan grunted.

If they bribed Milena's room-mate with the promise of a bunch of flowers or a bottle of vodka maybe she would let them into the shop before it officially opened, before the queues formed.

So, after three years of waiting his patience had been rewarded. His trumpet had finally arrived. Jan worked for the local fire brigade. It was his duty every day to play the mid-day time signal for live broadcast by national radio. Every day at twelve he would open the wooden shutters on the church tower in the ancient capital city and send forth the wailing Call to Arms over the busy market place down below. Although nobody ever saw him at his work, he liked to think that he was something of a celebrity.

There were historical reasons for the trumpet call. During the thirteenth century the town had been besieged by Tartars. The watchman, whose duties included keeping an eye open for fires – hence the connection with the local fire brigade – had seen the Tartar horde approaching, but in the middle of his alarm call had been struck in the throat by an arrow. He died with his call unfinished. Afterwards, when the Tartars had retreated, the alarm was adapted to include a peculiar abrupt finish in tribute to this lone watchman. Over the years the call had become an expression of national will, a sort of independence cut short, truncated. 'Yes,' the call proclaimed, 'in spite of everything, we're still here.' But this particular day was special. Today was the Thirtieth Anniversary of the Victory over Fascism. Today the trumpet call would signify not the victory over the long departed Tartars, but the resurrection of the state at the end of the war. An ambiguous gesture because that victory had also been a victory for the Red Army. The careerist boss of local radio had insisted that his station was essential to the celebrations.

The trumpet players had drawn lots for the honour of the broadcast, and Jan's triumph in the lottery was now crowned by the arrival of the trumpet. His old instrument he kept in a cloth bag which lay at the foot of the steps to the church tower. He was ashamed of it. It was very ancient and battered, and most of the lacquer had flaked away to reveal the dull grey metal underneath. Jan had pulled it from a huge pile of abandoned fluggelhorns and glockenspiels in the ruins opposite the town hall in the spring of 1945. It had been left behind by the retreating Germans as they fled the approach of the Red Army. Although it had a good rounded tone and a fine easy action, the trumpet was embossed with a huge Swastika enamelled in black and red. Jan had tried to lever it away, saw it off with a hacksaw, even to file in flat. But without effect. The Swastika remained as bright and prominent as on that first day.

After coffee Jan brightened up a little. He had been unhappy about celebrating the country's independence on a Nazi trumpet, but now it seemed he would have a People's trumpet. His headache eased a little.

He pulled on his trumpeter's traditional costume: long red trousers, a white shirt with a ruffled collar and cuffs, long red and black jacket with slashed sleeves. The red cavalier's hat with the long peacock feather he always kept at the church, with his trumpet. He pulled on his fireman's overcoat and cap. Outside it was still dark. In the distance they could hear the wheels of the first tram squealing along curved rails.

Jan bought a bunch of carnations at a roadside kiosk. They hammered on the door of the music shop, but there was no answer. They peered through the windows, but there was no light in the back room either. They stood on the steps stamping their feet and shuffling the snow about with the toes of their boots. Across the street a sign proclaimed 'A Strong Child Equals a Strong Nation.'

'Do we just wait?' said Jan.

'We could go and see Jacek at the Café. He'll give us a drink at least.'

'At this hour?'

Jan snorted and threw the bunch of flowers into the gutter. Their red was vivid against the grey snow.

Jacek, the Café manager opened the door to them, slipping in his false teeth as he did so.

'My wife is away, so I'm in charge for a couple of days. Great Aunt died. Something like that. Anyway, it's my show while she's gone. Marta, come on out here! We have guests!'

A thin blonde with mussy hair and blurred make-up appeared. She was wearing Jacek's overcoat, but was clearly naked underneath. Jacek took her hand and kissed it.

'My dear little mouse, be so good as to fix us bread and pickles.'

'But I don't know where anything is . . .'

177

'My dear, neither do I. Do your best, eh?' He patted her bottom and pushed her from the room.

'By the end of the week she'll know where everything is . . . just like my wife.' He took a vodka bottle from the shelf and poured three generous tumblers.

They drank their first glass straight down. Marta brought bread and pickles. They munched in silence. Marta made coffee.

'Tell you what,' said Jacek over a third glass of vodka. 'When you get the trumpet, why don't you come back over here and have a bit of a warm up before you do the broadcast? I'll send for Old Józef. We can all have a drink.'

Old Józef was the third trumpeter in the team. Piotr and Jan were not keen to have Old Józef around – he got drunk too quickly, embarrassed everyone by complaining that standards had dropped since the war, and wore a rod full of ribbons and medals dangling from his raincoat lapel. He also sniffed endlessly. Jacek called him 'Silver-sleeves' but he was fond of the old man and loved to hear tales of his good-old bad-old days.

Jan and Piotr buttoned up their coats, kissed Marta's hand and began the return journey to the music shop. It was daylight. The wind had dropped and snow was falling.

They picked their way over the fresh snow past a demolition gang at work on an old tenement building. A coalman with a horse and cart loudly insisted that he had to deliver an order of ten bags to the basement of the fast disappearing tenement. They paused to savour the row for a while. The coalman brought the exchange to an abrupt end by dumping the coal on the pavement and yelling at the foreman:

'There you are. I've done my job, the delivery is made. Now you sort it out.'

'Isn't our communism wonderful? Sometimes I think I am in a play,' said Jan. 'It's like as if it doesn't mean anything.'

'Oh it means something all right,' Piotr muttered. 'It's just that we don't know what.'

They walked on, weaving only slightly.

'With a bit of luck Jacek will be too involved with the girl. He'll forget Józef.'

Someone shouted across the street to them:

'There's bananas in the Delicatessen, boys. Better get in the queue quick.'

'Sod that,' said Jan quietly. 'Why should I stand in a queue? What have I got a wife for?'

As soon as the door to the music shop was un-bolted the waiting crowd rushed in like grit into a vacuum. Behind the counter there stood a glossy pile of Czechoslovak Country and Western albums, almost as high as the shop assistant. People were waving fistfuls of paper money. When Jan finally got the trumpet in his hands he battered his way out holding the trumpet case before him like a ram. Jan felt the alcohol had crept up on him. His vision was a little blurred, noises boomed in his ears.

They were crossing behind the demolition site towards the Café when they saw Marta. A bruise was just beginning to darken the underside of her jaw.

'Hit you did he?' said Piotr.

'His wife came back. The bitch.'

She was already walking away when Jan suggested that she come with them for a drink. She turned on her heel and spat at them.

'Men! Animals.' She ran across the uneven snow.

Old Józef appeared in the Café doorway. A bottle of vodka poked from his coat pocket.

'Nice mess, eh? Better not go in just now. Leave Jacek and his missus to sort things out, you know? Anyway,' he said, patting his coat pocket. 'I have a bottle, and that's the main thing, eh?'

Old Józef gave a phlegmy laugh and the three trumpeters turned to saunter. They had nearly an hour before the time signal. They found a sheltered space among the half-demolished apartment blocks. Under a sign that proclaimed 'Marx-Leninism – the Victory Flag of Our Epoch' they sat and opened the vodka.

'The new trumpet!' said Old Józef and took a long swig.

They passed the bottle from hand to hand and Old Józef began to tell a tale of the fighting on the road to Berlin. His breath made white clouds in the winter air. Eventually he paused.

'A great moment in the history of the nation. An honour, the moment when we look around at the work of reconstruction and remember why we are here . . .'

'Oh yes,' said Jan. 'And why are we here?'

Old Józef did not hear the question.

'Stabbed in the back by our allies, we was, every time . . .'

Piotr focused on his watch. Twenty minutes to go. They set off towards the market place, Old Józef clutching the nearly empty bottle. They paused for breath under the stern bronzed gaze of a statue – some long dead national poet that none of them had read. A farmer had hitched his horse and cart to the statue. Piotr looked at his watch. Ten to the hour. They would have to hurry.

They stumbled through the church doorway, unlocked the entrance to the tower, rattled and reeled their way up the two hundred and fifty steps to the broadcasting chamber. At the wooden ladder that marked the final stage of the ascent they paused, blowing hard. Jan took out his new trumpet, and polished it. Old Józef, swaying perilously close to the stair-well, said:

'The nation awaits your call.' He took a swig from the bottle.

They started up the ladder. Jan got wedged in the hatch. As he wrenched himself free he fell on the trumpet and dented the bell. He cursed. Piotr sat nearby. He pulled out Jan's old trumpet from its place in the corner and stripped off its cotton wrappings. The swastika gleamed hard and dull against the grey metal. Down below Old Józef wiped his nose on his sleeve:

'When the green light is on . . . when the green light is on . . .'

Piotr turned a glassy eye towards the wall panel. The green light started blinking.

'Jan! It's time. Thirty seconds . . .'

Jan vomited and slid sideways to the floor. The green light stopped blinking and the red light shone steadily. The broadcast had begun. They were on the air. Then Piotr jammed the ceremonial feathered hat on his head, picked up the Nazi trumpet and hauled himself to his feet. He staggered to the wooden shutter overlooking the market place and swung it open. The square unfolded beneath him.

A small crowd had gathered. They carried a banner that read: 'Under the Guidance of the Party we are Achieving the Economic Progress Set Forth at the Seventh Party Congress.'

Sweat broke out on his forehead. He raised the trumpet, but instead of the famous Call to Arms there came only a faint 'parrrp'. He leaned against the shutter, frowned and tried again. The first few notes struggled out, but he ran out of breath and the call ended not in limitation of a throat pierced by a Tartar arrow, but in a strange 'ssshhhppp'.

As Piotr began a third attempt he realised someone else was playing too, a bleary parody, a completely independent assault on the Call to Arms, raucous, jazzy and hopeless. Jan, lying on his side was blowing into the new trumpet with all his might. The effort was too much. Jan passed out, the trumpet clattered to the floor.

In the stair-well Old Józef was singing loudly: 'Still Poland is not lost as long as we are living . . .'

Below the crowd were craning their necks at the tower. Policemen were running towards the church.

'Oh Hell,' said Piotr.

The red broadcast light was still on.

SATURDAY IN THE 'SAC

Alan Beard

Alan Beard was born in Tewkesbury, Gloucestershire. His short stories have appeared in various magazines and journals including 'Cosmopolitan', 'Panurge', 'Critical Quaterly' and 'London Magazine'. Married with two daughters, he now lives in Birmingham.

SATURDAY IN THE 'SAC was first broadcast on Radio 4, read by Anthony Jackson.

SATURDAY IN THE 'SAC

This Saturday is different from the start: when we come to there's no Philip Schofield going on downstairs and no stream of hot water being used, no yells, no music, no arguments.

'The kids are out,' I say to Denise, 'how about coffee in bed?' I don't say breakfast, neither of us eat it. Coffee and a fag. 'I'll bring an ashtray up.'

'The shopping,' she calls. 'We've done it,' I shout from the stairs. Housework, gardening, fixing the bathroom, shovelling the catshit from our entry. Always something, but she's saying yes more these days and when I get back her face is warm from sleep still. We sit there legs out in front of us talking of our childhoods. I spent mine here in 'Oxford Place, Cul-de-Sac' – I say it like I used to as a child, when I'd reel off the full address, ending with 'the Universe'. Dee's was spent a mile or two away. Two weekend sounds recall her childhood – the bells of three churches competing, and the Saturday market at 6 p.m.: the stacking of scaffolding, tarpaulin into the backs of vans. We haven't done this for so long, chatted like this, all kids and favourite TV programmes you can't miss, so I'm wondering how it will turn out. I can feel her soften with nostalgia as we talk and I reach out from our pasts to her breast and she moves so my hand slips further and further down.

So Saturday begins. There's nothing on this weekend besides a trip to Denise's mother, Sunday. The pull-out table and place mats with old cars on them. The home-made pineapple cake for afters which I will say is 'deli-lish-us', a word stumble I made twenty-odd years ago at my first meal in that house.

185

The kids bored. Her dad and I might slip out to the pub, walking through streets still full of bells. But Saturday looked like gardening, sunbathing – hopefully – with a can or two, checking the pools. Later a film with – how do you pronounce it? – Cherie Lunghi in it. When the kids do return noisy as ever we are up singing 'She was just 17, you know what I mean', but soon TV, music upstairs and Louise's friends coming by drive me out into the garden. The usual Saturday in the weak sun, or else real cold that passes for summer. The usual: cutting brambles, considering how Dee's warm bra-marked flesh would feel through the creased pair of gardening gloves and whether she would object to me finding out. Gagging as I shovel up catshit and bury it while the sun slips higher and burns away cloud. Leaning on the fence talking to Brian, he still wearing an anorak with 'Fat Willy' on the back. He's recently out of a job, and putting on a brave face – a throat laugh that goes on too long, a grin that stays, as when his wife upped and took the kids with her and people who didn't know called 'All right Brian!'

He tells me old Barry Moore's house ('Lionel' to us kids) has been boarded up, padlocked and grilled. I picture a slice of house in a toaster. Christ didn't I hear the council making that racket this morning? Working on a Saturday, must think we're bad. Kids – not Louise or Blake he adds quickly – are already there, spraying and smashing. I'll give 'em child abuse. Brian getting warm enough to unzip.

Then on this Saturday when everything seems to happen, music beginning to blow from every open window – Blake's – a seagull drops into Brian's garden, side of his pond and stabs out the goldfish one by one. Bloated, it falls in. A seagull with indigestion in a 2' by 2' pond, no response to my neighbour's shouts and hand claps. 'I wouldn't mind,' Brian says, 'but we're nowhere near the fucking sea.'

And what's this my daughter's saying to me an hour later, make-up looking weird, saying to me of her friend, 'She earns £200 a week on them chat line things and what do I get: £7 a day on stupid Community Industry.'

Seven pounds a week was my first wage and I know this can't be right thirty years later and think nothing much is right thirty years later though we all thought it would be. I feel for her – her hair making her look like something left out in the wind, but 'Those things aren't right,' I say. 'Anyway you're only sixteen.'

'She's seventeen, but she passes for older,' she says as if this makes a difference, 'I don't look it do I?'

She wears a black and white mini which reminds me of the sixties, reminds me of Denise, but Lou's thinner. I thought at one time 'anorexic' but she – and Denise – say she isn't.

I go in after that to Blake's gatling-gun rap music – at his age.

The rest of the day comes blue, bluer, bluest as the temperature rises. It's maybe the first of many such days, or more likely a one-off. All day I'm in and out of the house, getting out of it in the cooler front room looking out of the bay at the sky, blue fingers dipping down among the houses. The city centre like a fortress in a haze away to the left.

The houses round here have that grey pebbledash which cracks and falls off in slices. Stub of lawn at the front, longer at the back. Not as bad as some places – a towerblock, say – but ageing is always a problem. Not as bad as Brian makes out, I always thought, but it's looking worse than I've ever seen it in the glare of light. They used to cut the grass in the middle, place to play games in my youth, but now it's overgrown with thistles, mounds of rubbish appearing and earth and grass, and flowering weeds. Young kids like tunnelling in it. Today one kid runs round and round the green, now precariously on the kerb, now off. Alexandra Stadium to him. The kids all wear baseball caps these days, American slang – Blake. (And very young girls get their hair permed – Louise.) 'Look,' I say to him when he appears slack-clothed from his music-drenched room, 'why don't you go out on a day like this. Or help in the garden?' He goes out.

When I look out later I see he's only got as far as the boarded-

187

up house. The end one at the neck, the exit/entrance to the cul-de-sac, a bit bigger than the others, an extra bedroom and a side garden with a tree. Denise used to go by saying 'Covet, covet.' For as long as I remember it was occupied only by Barry Moore, who'd always looked the same to me: huge black eyebrows and hanks of grey hair either side of a small head (though in forty years his appearance must have changed?). Lately he'd taken to stopping me and muttering some stuff about a football team I used to play in. It was a daily ritual, always on my way home from work, my gate in sight and with weariness instead of blood circulating in me I'd nod him on, nod him on. I was some link to his past: we were the two remaining original occupants of 'Oxford Place, Cul-de-Sac'. Then, last week, he died.

I walk down the outdoors for some cans, but more to see what's going on around that house (there's graffiti already on one boarded-up window – I LOVE MYSELF), and to have a glance at Blake. His gang are chucking stones into the middle of the green where somebody has made a little sculpture of bricks, tins and lino. At least there are no glue bags in sight. 'Pack it in,' I shout at them to no effect, although Blake stops. He nods at me like some distant acquaintance. I remember practising with a ball out on the green when they used to cut it, trying to teach him to kick with both feet. That was my trouble – I got into the school team, left midfield, but couldn't progress because I was too one-footed.

To the outdoors, looking forward to the beer, having cans in the fridge for later; Denise'll have one with me. The sunglasses of the Marlboro ad reflect a landscape not of the flyover that rises in the air way above our heads, but of somewhere hotter. Desert. That outcrop of rock Indians always hide behind.

Coming back there's a jagged hole in the empty house door. Axed through by the look, padlock still holding the frame in place. There's a boy in the tree, breaking off twigs and small branches and throwing them down. I don't recognise him. No sign of Blake.

Out the back with the beer and a lie in the sun with the newspaper. Sounds from the 'Sac echoing down our entry and the occasional squawks from the fat seagull next door send me into a snooze over next week's TV. I'm woken by Denise saying the Australian results are on and I should check them. She's pulled out a deck chair and has on a bikini top and shorts. I wonder how long she's been there, and touch her neck to see how warm she is.

'Louise phoned. She's staying with 'Lex.' Alex? Isn't that the name of the friend she told me about in the garden, the one who speaks dirt down the phone? I can't help imagining what she might say. But Denise says at least she phoned, and I feel relieved it isn't worse news.

Marian draws up in a K-reg car, on her way somewhere. Dressed up to show off to Denise and Louise (the two eeses, she calls them). She worries about her car, she wonders how we can live here, why don't we move now both of us are earning? Of course we've thought about it and might still, have to see how secure these jobs are. 'It's not that bad,' I say. She asks is something going on because half the street's milling about outside.

Then she settles into some office gossip, they both work at police headquarters in the city. 'Anita says, "I suppose you don't get that problem do you, at your age, the uniformed men eyeing you up." Cheek.' I see the two turn and wrap themselves in slanderous conversation.

I look outside for Blake. Three sets of music come from around the 'Sac. Older men in unbuttoned shirts lounge on someone's steps in the sun. After Marian goes we have a laugh, but Dee is thinking life can be good for a divorcee maybe and I need to touch her and see her eyes look at me square again. Of course when I sit next to her Blake drifts in.

'What's going on out there?'

'Nutten.'

Brian comes round too, should we call the police? Apparently they were round earlier. Brian says we should at least get Blake away, and although I think it'll come to nothing, we decide it might be for the best. I ring my brother across the city and he says fine, Blake can stay. He will enjoy it, we think, thrashing his cousin at Sonic Hedgehog ('Sonic the Hedgehog,' he corrects me). But he's reluctant and we bribe him – Dee's idea – with a stop at the drive-in McDonalds, not long open, and still of interest to him.

We drive round on the ring road to the big yellow M. I give our orders to the hatted girl behind the automatic window and moan to wife and son. 'America!'

'This used to be a cinema.' I say this every time we pass here, and say it now to tease Blake. Denise and I swap titles of films we'd seen when we were 'courting'. 'Barbarella.' 'Midnight Cowboy.' '2001.'

'Your mother was a film fanatic, we were the only couple that didn't snog.'

When we get the order we drive to the car park, eat our Big Macs and watch other cars come and go. It's still blue outside. I share a milkshake with Dee. We can't resist cigarettes. We, who love smoke curling from our mouths too much and forget about the smell and the stain and the lung damage. We'll reform, we'll stop, we'll do it we say – and the years pass.

'Open the window then.' Blake disgusted.

We drop him off all right and drive home feeling light. 'Shall we stop off for some more cans?' I ask. Which we do.

Then, when we're nearing a lane I know, that loops down behind a garage and ends at the canal, I say, 'Do you want to park up?' Denise laughs: it was what was said after those cinema nights when, still discussing the film, she gave me what I missed in those back rows. We sit silent for a while at this unexpectedness, and then re-live a night long ago with its early slow caress, and fiddling with clothes. She ends up on top, not moving much, jammed on to me, head bent with the roof. We swap teenage giggles, hold each other steady. When I've come I notice her eyes looking down on me and wonder if she's seeing all the days since that first time in the car – and what she makes of it all. Us.

We come apart slowly, in stages. We're happy as we rejoin the road. But blue light and sirens, a fire engine and police vans, force us to park up again. And when we get moving a helicopter comes steadily above – with a searchlight coning out shop fronts.

It swings over rooftops. We turn off and there is the rocking machine, balanced at an angle on its cone of light, above our corner.

The police are erecting a barrier and say we can't get in the 'Sac now. Overturned cars are across the entrance. I recognise Brian's. I look out at bands of policemen, shields resting on the vans, milling amongst the vehicles.

'What will you do?' Denise asks across me. She knows the policeman from work.

'Take it easy. See what happens.'

He won't tell us much about what's happening in there. Just keeps advising us to go somewhere else. We drive off but decide to circle back and come into the estate another way. Denise reckons Pat will let us through her back garden – if the police aren't there – and we can get into Brian's and then our own.

Pat thinks we're mad to go back – 'Stay here the night!' We hurry through the gardens and although its not yet quite dark I misjudge a jump and get a sogger in Brian's empty pool. No sign of him.

When we get into our place I see the Cherie Lunghi film finishing – we've left the television on. My insiders are sliding as we go to the front window and stand side by side to watch what is happening down the 'Sac.

A whole industry going on out there, people buzzing around Barry Moore's. Not only kids as you might expect, but the adults who'd finally had enough of waiting for the break, of keeping themselves and their kids occupied, and now organise them in the dismantling of the house.

People carry out doors, chopped-up stairs in bundles, window frames and skirting boards. They throw them on the fire on the green, half the size of a house, and boosted by unwanted furniture, fences, the tree in lengths and set on fire with syphoned petrol, probably from the overturned cars. Flame bearing heat to every surrounding window shoots up. This on a day still hot and light pouring down from a helicopter. A cheer goes up as the helicopter moves up and across out of the way of a high reaching flame. That's done it, I think, the police will

191

pile in now. I'm wondering what to do, and notice something familiar on the TV screen. 'Look' I say to Denise. I'm seeing what I never thought I would see. Live TV pictures from our corner.

THE RIGHT SET

Nigel Williams

Nigel Williams was born in Cheshire in 1948, educated at Highgate School and Oriel College, Oxford, and is married with three children. He is the author of a number of television and stage plays. His books include *My Life Closed Twice*, *Jack be Nimble*, *Star Turn*, *Witchcraft*, (for which he wrote the television adaptation), and a highly successful series of novels: *The Wimbledon Poisoner*, *They Came from SW19*, and most recently, *East of Wimbledon*. He is editing *The Picador Book of Humour*, and, not surprisingly, lives near Wimbledon.

THE RIGHT SET was broadcast in three parts on Radio 4. The reader was Nigel Anthony.

THE RIGHT SET

'Thirty all!' said Norman, in an accent that was clearly not his own. Norman owned an off-licence. Unkind people in Wimbledon maintained he put two pounds extra on a bottle of Beaujolais, simply because he talked like a member of the Royal family.

Why, thought Henry, am I always playing on the next court to Norman? He is the person I hate most in Wimbledon – or rather, one of the people.

Norman always knew the score. No one else did, or for that matter understood why he should always have such a detailed knowledge of it. It rarely did him credit. And Norman weighed about fifteen stone. This didn't stop him from wearing tennis whites, or from thrusting his buttocks out as if about to solicit sexual favours from the assorted dentists, lawyers, computer salesmen and graphic designers who filled the courts of the Wimbledon Heights Tennis Club at this hour of a Sunday morning.

Why, thought Henry grimly, did they call it the Wimbledon Heights Tennis Club? It was confusing. One of these days, Bjorn Borg was going to turn up and ask to play a few sets.

It wasn't Bjorn Borg these days was it? Henry couldn't remember the names of the tennis players any more. He was getting old. He paced inconclusively up and down the base line, trying to remember why he had joined the club in the first place. It wasn't even in Wimbledon. Anyone who knew anything about SW19 – and Henry was a world expert on the subject – knew that every single figure out on the courts this Sunday was at least fifty yards inside Southfields. Which was probably why the subscription rates to the club were so low. That, of course was why he had joined. Henry started to bounce the ball in front of him, trying to look like a man who had a serve on which

195

he could concentrate. He was only playing his daughter but it was still important to win. Maisie didn't look like a player on whom anyone would put money. She wasn't even putting on a show of attention. As far as Henry could make out, she was not bending at the waist, the way you were supposed to when waiting for one of his killer serves. Not that you would have been able to tell if she *had* been bending at the waist. Erect or crouching, Maisie presented five feet eight of concentrated flab to the world. Her nickname at school was Jabba the Hut. It was partly to try and reduce her weight that Henry forced her out onto the courts: someone had to supervise her exercise with the utmost care. They had tried to send her, on her own, to the Lime View Health Club. It was only after she had been going for three months that Henry and Elinor found out she was spending all her time in the restaurant.

'Come on Daddy!' she said, 'let's get it over with!'

They had suggested she go to a plastic surgeon for Spot Fat Reduction. But Maisie, once she had seen the menu of possibilities, had demanded receding chin correction, eyebag and eyelid replacement, breast enlargement and a particular kind of nose job that would have cost about as much as Henry's car.

Henry threw the ball high in the air and whacked it across the net. It bounced inside the inner court, and bounced past Maisie's ear. She looked after it resentfully: 'That's not fair, you're supposed to hit it *to* me!'

What made it worse was the fact that Norman was playing 'Steel Thighs' Jessup, the Balham architect who had once boasted that he could take on the entire club with both hands tied behind his back. He looked, this morning, as if he was trying this technique out on Norman. Jessup was not in the traditional pre-service position. Both right and left arm, and, presumably, racket, were draped, yearningly, over his buttocks. With a shock, Henry realised that the star of the Wimbledon Heights Tennis Club was doing some kind of breathing exercise. The combination of Jessup's performance and Norman's crouch made it look as if the two men were engaged in some complex mating ritual of the kind found in the pages of *A la Recherche du Temps Perdu*.

As he hit the next ball past Maisie's head, he saw both Norman and 'Steel Thighs', as if in deliberate synchronicity, turn their heads sharp left and leave them facing in that direction. Was this, wondered Henry, some new pre-match ritual enjoined on all serious members of the club? Following the line of their gaze he realised it was not. Coming round the side of the clubhouse, in immaculate tennis whites, dangerous looking tennis shoes and a couple of designer-made sweatbands, was a black man.

There had been, a few years back, a German member called Heinz, although he let his membership lapse after Henry did his Hitler moustache act in the bar late one night. There were rumours of a Chinaman called Ping Ho – although, even if he had paid his subscription the man had never actually dared show his face anywhere near the premises. But, as long as Henry had been playing there, the Wimbledon Heights Tennis Club had been one hundred per cent white. Or, to put it more accurately, thought Henry as he looked around the courts – one hundred per cent pink.

How had the man got through the front door, let alone past the selection committee? Peter Bates, Peter Pearse, Peter Piper and Peter Parker had given Henry a fairly nasty couple of hours at his interview. Peter Piper had asked him, several times, whether Farr was a Jewish name.

'Shurely shome mistake!' Norman was saying to 'Steel Thighs' as the black man made his way towards the one vacant court – on the other side of where he and Jessup were playing.

How had the man done it? Had he worn a disguise of some kind? Had he sent someone else along to the interview? Or had he, and this was entirely possible, simply wandered in off the streets? He didn't, to the obvious relief of almost everyone there, appear to have a partner. But this didn't seem to trouble him. He went to the base line of the empty court and from an elegant shoulder bag took out a plastic tube full of tennis balls, two rackets and a small bottle of mineral water. It was, thought Henry with some satisfaction, the beginning of the end. South Africa had fallen. Wimbledon's turn was bound to come. No one, as far as he could make out, was even pretending to play. All attention was focused on the tall, elegant stranger.

Under the watchful eyes of about thirty or forty Wimbledonians, the black man threw the ball high into the air, did a worryingly efficient dance-like step and with considerable force smashed the first of his balls hard into the net. The mood on the courts relaxed.

'It's long jumping they're good at!' said Norman, loudly, in Henry's direction. The stranger meanwhile, unperturbed, reached for his second ball. Maisie, her racket drooping from nerveless fingers, was staring at him with the kind of attention she usually reserved for the American Hot, served in the local Pizza Express. With the second ball he cleared the net but served out of court. With the third he achieved the kind of obvious ace that even 'Steel Thighs' would have been unable to return. With the next ball it was back into the net.

And so it went on. He seemed to have everything required to make a tennis player. He was tall. He was obviously fit. He could hit the ball very hard. When he served with any precision he was quite clearly of professional standard. But he seemed incapable of maintaining any degree of accuracy.

It was Norman, curiously enough, who was the first to offer him a game. Probably, thought Henry, because the strain of trying to work out who the stranger might be was unbearable.

'Peter Piper might have made a mistake!' he called to 'Steel Thighs', 'maybe the chap phoned up and asked if he could try out the courts or something. Some of them sound quite English over the phone!'

The stranger did sound very English. He had the kind of natural, aristocratic accent that Norman had never quite managed to imitate correctly. For some inexplicable reason, Henry thought it sounded vaguely familiar.

'I'd love a game old chap!' said the man. 'Shall we play doubles?'

Norman and 'Steel Thighs' seemed to like this idea.

'You could play with Henry!' said 'Steel Thighs', adding under his breath that this would be the equivalent of forcing the darkie to run around the court in football boots. Maisie seemed very keen to watch her father being humiliated and, against his will, Henry went over to join the stranger.

'Henry Farr!' said Henry. The black man seemed to hesitate slightly. For a moment Henry could have sworn he had seen him somewhere before as well. But this wasn't possible. There were no black people in the solicitors for whom he worked, and no black parents at the expensive school to which they had sent Maisie. The only black people he ever saw were on the street or on television.

'Call me . . . Julian,' the stranger said, eventually.

Norman gave a puckered little smile: 'Nice little serve you have there!'

'When it goes in,' said Julian.

It was at this point that 'Steel Thighs' suggested fifty pounds on the match. The speed with which the stranger accepted, reminded Henry one of those hustlers who frequent American films.

'Have you been a member long?' said 'Steel Thighs' as he and Norman re-grouped on the other side of the net.

'Do you have to be a member?' said Julian.

Norman and 'Steel Thighs' exchanged glances.

'Let's have the game anyway' said Norman, 'and we can point you at the selection committee after you and Henry have thrashed us!'

This seemed the perfect, diplomatic solution to the stranger's arrival: there was after all, as Emily Pratt said to Mabel Lawley, a waiting list.

'Steel Thighs' served first to Julian. Once he had recovered from his surprise that Henry's partner managed to return, Jessup forced the ball over towards Henry. While Henry was still trying to work out where the ball might land, Julian bounded over to his left, flicked it back over the net and watched impassively as fourteen stone of off-licence proprietor Norman thundered off in hopeless pursuit.

'Love fifteen!' said Henry, who hadn't been able to make such a remark to 'Steel Thighs' before. He sneered slightly as he prepared to receive the architect's serve, already under the delusion, as so often in doubles matches, that he had played some significant part in gaining the last point.

There was the familiar blur of Jessup's arm, the kind of grunting noise Henry normally associated with visits to the lavatory and somewhere ahead of him the sound of something hitting tarmac. Henry looked around for a moving tennis ball but didn't see one.

'Fifteen all!' said Jessup.

'Bad luck!' said Henry's partner, 'he has a mean serve!'

'Steel Thighs' Jessup allowed himself a small smile.

'Have you ever played professionally?' said the black man to Jessup – which, some people said, was the question Jessup had been waiting forty years for.

The first two points more or less set the pattern of the game. The only points that he and Julian lost were when Henry was serving or receiving service – apart from two double faults served by Norman. Julian's service was so terrifyingly hard and accurate that for a time Henry believed he actually *was* the first tennis hustler to be sighted in Wimbledon. Even 'Steel Thighs' was powerless against it. But the black man's manner was so unfailingly courteous. If he was a tennis hustler he had managed the final test of the good con man – he made his victims enjoy being robbed. He was always quiet, gentle and discreet, especially at the moment of victory. He resisted the temptation to leap over the net and shout 'Give me five bro!' every time he slammed another ball past the racket of Ronald Jessup, a man who was known to put his architect's business before his wife and his tennis a long way ahead of either of them. As the match proceeded, most of the games on the other courts ground to a halt. Henry heard Ella 'I was at RADA' Makepiece whisper to a friend that this was the most exciting match the Wimbledon Heights Tennis Club had ever seen. A crowd of spectators – some from the clubhouse, some from the remaining games in progress – gathered to watch 'Steel Thighs' serve to Julian. With a shock, Henry realised that the score was 5–3 in favour of the architect and the off-licence manager. Jessup was serving for the match.

'Go for it pardner!' said Henry in a tough, no-nonsense manner. Everyone looked at him rather curiously. 'Steel Thighs' tossed the ball high in the air and, creasing his piggy little eyes with concentration, prepared to vindicate the honour of the club.

Henry was amazed that he and the black man were only 5–3 down. And he was not the only one. Peter Piper observed to Peter Parker, later, that this was the only time any player forced to partner Henry had ever managed to win a single game. It was often said at the club that even two competent players playing with Henry might stand a chance of losing against one determined opponent. Indeed 'playing Henry' had become a kind of folk expression to indicate any kind of disaster up to and including death.

Henry crouched with what he hoped was professional keenness, as 'Steel Thighs' wound his racket back, hopped neatly to his left and smashed the ball over the net. It wasn't just that he hit it hard. He hit it, thought Henry, with the kind of passion that suggested that Julian had just asked to marry his daughter. It wasn't only hard: it was well placed and mercilessly well timed. For a moment, it seemed as if Julian might not be able to return it. But he moved left across the court and caught it with a meaty, satisfying backhand that sent it back, low and sweet and marked for the attention, not of 'Steel Thighs' but of his less talented partner. Somehow or other Norman, whose face was now the colour of his overpriced claret, got behind the ball. Or at least alongside it. Sliding along the surface of the court he managed to put the rim of his racket between the projectile and the ground. It bounced off at a crazy angle, rose high in the air and started on a downward path towards a spot three yards to the left of Henry.

'I'll get it!' called the black man in clear, reasonable tones. And he started without any particular appearance of hurry to amble towards Henry's half of the court. The ball was still about twenty feet in the air.

'I think,' said Henry, 'that I can cope with this one!'

'Are you absolutely sure about that?' said Julian.

'I think I have the thing under control! I am not a *total* incompetent you know!'

The ball seemed to be taking an amazingly long time to get back to earth.

'If you're sure.' said Julian. With a shock Henry realised the black man was signalling to him. Julian was pointing at the ball which was now about six feet above his head. He seemed to be offering to take it off Henry's hands. But it was already too late. Henry whirled his racket round, swatted the air feebly and watched the ball drop about three yards away from him and bounce solemnly away across the court.

'Game I think gentlemen!' said 'Steel Thighs' allowing himself another small smile.

People at the club said they had never seen a man with such perfect manners as Julian. He strode manfully up to the net and with the air of someone who had been expecting just such a result produced a fifty pound note, which he handed to 'Steel Thighs' with a slight bow. Then he turned to Henry, who was giving the watching crowd his 'I pay my subscription, don't I?' look.

'Bad luck partner!' he said in beautifully modulated tones, 'I was rather hogging the ball. You played a very honest game!' Afterwards, some people said it was Henry who had asked the black man to the clubhouse for a drink.

But, in fact, it was 'Steel Thighs' who asked Julian for a drink and 'Steel Thighs' who, over a half of lager, asked him whether he would be interested in joining. The fact was that the Balham architect hadn't had such a satisfying victory since he beat 'Hairy' Duvalier, the former French professional at an exhibition match designed to raise money for Juliana Barnes's hip replacement in 1989. And 'Steel Thighs' was, as he pointed out to close friends, nearly forty. He was looking around for a successor.

'I'll be honest,' he told 'Jumpy' Prang the former RAF pilot, 'I hold no particular brief for the average black man. But for me tennis comes first. The man's a damn good sportsman. I don't care if he's bright green.'

When 'Steel Thighs' made his offer, Henry expected Peter Piper, Peter Pearse, Peter Bates and Peter Parker, who were all in the bar, to take him outside and have a quiet word. But they, too, seemed to wish to adopt the stranger. After 'Steel Thighs' had bought them all a drink with Julian's fifty pounds, they agreed to waive the usual membership committee meeting.

And after 'Steel Thighs' had bought them all a second drink, Peter Piper said it was nice to see a few new faces around the place and he personally would stand up for any man's right to be a tennis player first and everything else second. No one asked him what he meant by this.

There was only one moment when people said they should have suspected something. When Peter Pearse asked Julian for his address the black man said he lived in Heathview Gardens. Henry knew a thing or two about the street map of Wimbledon: 'Don't you mean – Heathview *Crescent* old man?'

Julian smiled and said of course he did. There was, as Henry pointed out to anyone prepared to listen, a Heathview Gardens in Morden and two of them in Raynes Park. It was an easy mistake to have made.

But, when Peter Pearse asked him how he would be paying, Julian said 'by banker's order'. And when the first monthly payment arrived it was from a branch of Coutts in central London. The name on the account was J. Thomson. There was nothing unusual in that. Except, as Peter Parker pointed out, this was the first time that any of them had been given a clue as to Julian's surname.

'I've seen him before somewhere!' said Henry, 'I could swear I've seen him before. Or heard his voice or something . . .'

But no one listened to Henry. No one ever listened to Henry.

'Care for the next dance?' said Julian.

'I'd love to!' said Amanda Jessup.

There had never been, thought Henry morosely, a club member as popular as Julian. He stood his round. He was a good listener. In fact he hardly ever opened his mouth to speak. He was always offering people lifts in his BMW. He was clearly going to be the star of the Summer Ball which traditionally took place at the beginning of Wimbledon Fortnight.

'We'll have to be off soon!' said 'Steel Thighs' Jessup. His wife gave a brief, pained smile and moved onto the floor with Julian. Julian put one hand to her waist and, holding her right hand lightly with his left, started to sway easily to the music.

'Love fifteen!' said Henry to his daughter as they made their way back from the bar. They found themselves a table in the corner. Maisie, as usual, was drinking pints of lager. She took a deep swig from her glass and gave a ladylike belch.

'Jessup,' she said, in tones of some satisfaction, '*hates* Julian!'

'Just five minutes now!' called 'Steel Thighs' to his wife. She looked at him over Julian's upper right arm. The upper right arm that had in the last few months taken nearly two hundred service games off the Balham architect.

'Don't be petty darling!' she called, 'we're having fun! I've got the hots for Hunky Jules!'

Julian gave a slight, almost weary nod of the head.

'Love thirty!' said Maisie, 'Julian leads by two games to love in the first set!'

One game, thought Henry as he groped for his double Scotch, probably referred to an incident earlier in the evening when Julian had put 'Steel Thighs' right on a point of fact about the rules governing the tie-break. And what was the other? As if in answer to his unspoken thought, Maisie said,

'Julian always starts one game ahead because he's so amazing and you're all such horrible racists!'

She was always saying things like this in the club bar. Usually in a very loud voice.

Over in the corner, 'Steel Thighs' could be heard: 'Who is he anyway? Why doesn't he say who he is or where he's from?'

Everyone knew to whom he was referring. Julian was known in club circles as the Mystery Man. He never discussed his life outside the club. It was as if such a thing didn't exist. He always arrived, and left, in tennis whites. He never used the showers – greatly to the relief of 'Verwoerd' Hughes, the club accountant, who told his friends in the Frog and

Ferret that he had no wish to be 'overwhelmed by the man's equipment'.

There was also the question of his briefcase.

He always arrived carrying a plastic bag in which were his tennis balls (he had twenty of them), a towel, a small thermos, and a copy of some current reading matter. For the last three weeks, according to Maisie, he had been reading Antonia Byatt's *Possession*. But with the plastic bag he always had a small, black, leather briefcase. It was locked. Maisie had tried to open it three or four times. Once she had taken a small hammer to it while Julian was in the middle of a ten-game marathon with 'Steel Thighs,' at the end of which the defeated architect had had to be taken home in a taxi. But no one had ever seen what was inside.

And there were other, inexplicable things about his behaviour.

The way he leaned forward, very closely, when he was having one of those intimate conversations with club members. The way he would suddenly rise, in the middle of one such encounter and thrust himself across the table as if overcome with lust for the person with whom he was talking. The way he had talked one night when slightly drunk – the only such occasion – so wistfully and sadly of 'his treatment'.

'It's my treatment . . .' he had said to Toby 'Watch the Au Pair' Gutteridge, 'do you see . . . it's my treatment . . . ?'

Toby was of the opinion that Julian hadn't long to live. There were others who said he was a professional player trying to 'case out' the All England Lawn Tennis Club.

Amanda Jessup and Julian were dancing very closely. Over by the bar 'Steel Thighs' had ordered a double brandy. He was deep in conversation with Norman, who was about to start his third bottle of Beaujolais.

'I never minded them when they were bus conductors. But have you noticed that these days the bus conductors are *white*! The blacks are riding around in Rolls Royces, high on cocaine!'

Norman didn't attempt to test this judgement against his immediate experience. He nodded, in a way intended to convey fellow feeling, combined with a certain lack of interest. 'Monica Seles is a sloppy, sloppy player!'

'Steel Thighs' looked over towards the dance floor where Amanda was leaning her head against Julian's. He started to grind his teeth: 'Who is he? Who the hell *is* he? Whoever he is – he isn't who he says he is, is he?'

As Julian had never said who he was this was a hard statement to contradict. And no one anyway seemed prepared to take 'Steel Thighs' up on the point. Someone, as they often did at this stage of the evening, put on 'The Chicken Song' very loudly. Amanda started to rotate her thighs slowly and then thrust her pelvis forward, hard, at her partner. Julian, instead of looking round humorously at the rest of the club (which was how you were supposed to behave when Amanda Jessup did this to you) rotated his thighs back at her. Not only that. He put his right hand behind his head and gave a convincing pelvic thrust all of his own.

'How de doo di doo da!' said Peter 'Husband and Father' Winterson.

'Isn't he wondrous!' said Maisie.

Henry sank more of his scotch.

Everyone said afterwards that it was Julian's fault. That 'Steel Thighs' was by then drunk. That there must have been ways in which Jessup might have been calmed. But in the view of expert Jessup watchers there was nothing short of chloroform or a massive injection of valium in the left buttock that would have stopped 'Steel Thighs' – once the club secretary had made the mistake of putting on 'Lady in Red'. 'Lady in Red', as Jessup was always ready to explain was his and Amanda's favourite tune: 'When I hear it,' he was fond of saying, 'my belly turns to water. I can only think of Amanda. I think of what a great wife and mother she's been to me. I think of her body, and I remember she is the best preserved forty-eight-year-old woman I know. And I melt!'

During this number, Henry couldn't help noticing that Julian put both arms round Amanda's waist, moved his cheek close to hers and in the far gloom of the clubhouse, began to nibble her ear. Amanda, instead of responding with a forearm smash to

206

the face (as Ella Pearse declared she would have done) started to rub her right leg along the line of Julian's left thigh. Jessup's face darkened. His right hand went down to his own right thigh, considered by many to be his best feature, and he started with ominous calm to saunter over to his wife and her dancing partner. His lips were moving slowly but no one could hear what he was saying.

He moved through the dancers as 'Lady in Red' reached its wailing, desperate climax. All around him, husbands and wives were petting each other inexpertly in the gloom. And over by the wall Amanda had slipped her right hand inside Julian's elegant black jacket and was beginning to massage his left breast. Julian – a faraway look in his eyes – was allowing his own left hand to cup Mrs Jessup's ample buttocks. Just as 'Steel Thighs' came up to them, the black man began to knead Amanda's rear end and to align his handsome face a few inches above hers. Henry watched the architect nervously. This was the man who had broken Dennis Watson's arm after Watson had borrowed his racket press without asking permission. And Henry wasn't the only one watching the encounter. All over the darkened room, club members separated from their clinches, put down their drinks and breathed in slowly as they waited to see what would happen.

'Steel Thighs' waited until his wife had started to pucker her lips at the tall, handsome stranger before tapping him on the shoulder.

'Hands off my old lady sonny. She's only allowed chocolate at weekends!'

Julian turned round, with what seemed almost leisurely interest. Henry didn't see his left hand go out but 'Honky' Miller, who studied boxing, said it reminded him of Frank Bruno's 'flick'. It didn't seem to have the whole of the man's body weight behind it, but it must have landed on 'Steel Thighs'' nose with considerable force as the architect fell backwards into the darkness, his strong right hand flailing wildly up at his opponent. As blood started to course from Jessup's nose, 'Arthur' Du Cane, the club bore said: 'Steady on Sambo!'

Julian wheeled round. 'Chunky' Boyle, the film editor, pushed his common-law wife aside and, his face dark with anger, assumed the kind of boxing crouch usually seen in sporting prints of the eighteenth century.

'Come on then!' he muttered, 'come on then!'

Julian moved towards his opponent. 'Chunky' made a loose right jab at his face. But even while he was in the middle of doing this, the black man was giving him a high punch to the head followed by two short blows to the stomach. 'Chunky', whose work on a Hollywood epic about Louis Pasteur had been nominated, by his neighbours, for an industry award, made a noise like a punctured lilo and fell to the floor. Two committee members, Peter Piper and Peter Pearse, ran at Julian waving their arms. They, too, ended up on the floor. One of them as far as Henry could make out had sustained some form of spinal injury.

After that things went rather quiet, apart from Maisie: 'Zap the bastards!' she muttered into her lager.

Julian looked round at the assembled members of the Wimbledon Heights Tennis Club and said: 'I really am frightfully sorry. I was simply dancing with the man's wife.'

At this point Amanda Jessup burst into tears, went over to the father of her two children and started to wipe the blood from his face.

'I love you Monkey dear!' said 'Steel Thighs' in a loud voice. It was the first time he had used his pet name outside their bedroom in twenty-two years of marriage. Julian looked round at the assembled Wimbledonians, and with a brief, saddened laugh started towards the door.

It was only after he had gone, and after Peter Piper had been given back massage by Otto Kahn, the club osteopath, that someone noticed Julian's briefcase, on one of the chairs at the bar.

'Probably got a bomb in it!' said 'Chunky' Boyle who, like everyone else, had been given a free drink by the club secretary and was explaining how black boxers often threw low punches.

It was 'Steel Thighs' who suggested they open it: 'At least we'll find out who the bastard was!'

Everyone felt the use of the past tense was appropriate. It was clear that were he to show his face again he would not be welcome. Peter Pearse said that the committee would guarantee that if he came within fifty yards of the premises, they would break every bone in his body. At which Maisie muttered, 'If he doesn't break all yours first!'

But who was going to open it? Nobody seemed willing to take the risk. Henry looked away from the mysterious black bag, out into the Wimbledon night. Somewhere away in the distance he heard Julian's BMW roar into life and drive off up towards the village. He was clearly not coming back for it. Club member looked at club member. But no one moved. It was as if the briefcase, like its owner, had been sent to torment them. As if, for the first time in recorded history, the members of the Tennis Club had been confronted with something unique in Wimbledon – a moral dilemma.

Opening another man's property did not come easily to the membership of the tennis club. There was something about a man's briefcase that was sacred. Away from its owner, Julian's precious piece of luggage acquired an air of respectable mystery. It looked as if it might contain something important and official.

'Maybe,' said Arthur Du Cane, 'he worked for the government or something.'

'You can never tell,' said Maisie, 'they can have quite powerful connections these days!'

By the time a few more drinks had gone down everyone had convinced themselves that Julian was an undercover agent for the Atomic Energy Authority. Several people were prepared to swear that they had seen the briefcase chained to the man's wrist. Peter Pearse put his ear to it and announced that he could hear ticking. Then Amanda Jessup ran out onto the courts and would only come back inside after Pearse himself had told her he was joking, admitted the joke was in poor taste and publicly stated that although Julian had nibbled her ear Amanda had never laid a finger on the swine.

In the end Henry was deputed to open the case. 'Henry has a furtive look about him!' said off-licence Norman, 'he looks like a man who would know how to pick a lock or two!'

'I know –' said 'Steel Thighs', who had now recovered his composure and whose face no longer showed any traces of blood – 'we could get Maisie to sit on it!'

Everybody laughed. Henry picked up the case and, beckoning to his daughter went out on to the verandah. 'Anyone who wants to be implicated in the violation of Julian's privacy please follow me!' Nobody did.

Out on the verandah the summer air was sweet. The lights of the main road could be seen beyond the plane trees, and, beyond them, the dark spaces of Wimbledon Park. Somewhere further up the hill was the golf course, the common, and the green sweep of Surrey. Henry breathed in deeply, holding the briefcase at arms length.

'Shall we open it?'

'Of course!' said Maisie.

Taking a brooch from her blouse, she started to work its clasp carefully into the mechanism of the case's brass lock. She seemed to know what she was doing. At least, thought Henry, she had learned to do something useful at the Martha Collins Academy for Young Ladies. She made a quick thrust forward, pulled hard at the straps above the lock and slipped her hand inside.

'It's papers!' She pulled out forty or fifty typed sheets.

Henry felt a sudden qualm: 'I don't think we should . . .' But he moved over to his daughter's shoulder, as, under the yellow light on the clubhouse porch, Maisie read Julian's secret.

It was headed: *Racism in the Suburbs by Julian De Vere Thomson, a treatment for a fifty minute radio documentary in the 'Undercover London' spot*. Henry only read the first few words – 'Racial attitudes in white bourgeois society are, inevitably, covert and it is only by penetrating a classic fortress of reactionary racist attitudes – such as the Tennis Club – that we can . . .'

Maisie's mouth had opened like a fish's. She seemed to have read further than Henry.

'He had a tape recorder!' she was whispering, 'he's got a transcript of 'Chunky' Boyle talking to Norman. When he was drunk! They're discussing the average IQ of black immigrants!'

Henry gulped: 'That was where I'd heard his voice. On the radio!'

There was more than Julian's 'treatment' in the briefcase. At last Henry understood the meaning of the word. There was a small recorder and ten or fifteen of the tapes themselves, all of which amounted to unanswerable proof of the racial attitudes of the Wimbledon Heights Tennis Club. He had Julia MacEwan talking to Mary Seymour in frank and candid detail about 'the fearsome size of the negro races'. He had Peter Piper and Peter Pearse using the words 'chocco' and 'Sambo'.

He had a spectacular display of ignorance – medical, geographical and cultural – from 'Steel Thighs' in a taped conversation with Olga the ugly Estate Agent. It began with the words 'Is Julian a common name among our Caribbean brethren?' and then got a lot worse.

On the plastic box containing the tapes was written:

Only copy of highly confidential recordings. If found please return to Julian De Vere Thomson 'Undercover London' Free South London Radio SW19.

Maisie looked back into the clubhouse: 'This could do the club a great deal of damage!'

'You're right!' said Henry, 'you can't argue with your own voice on tape can you?'

'They might close the whole place down. You have to be very careful about being racist these days.'

Henry had certainly always been very discreet about it. He tiptoed nearer to the clubhouse and from the safety of the darkness peered in at the members. Inside 'Steel Thighs' was telling Norman how he had beaten Henry while having a conversation on his mobile-phone. Peter Piper was proposing to add the word 'British' to the club name on the board outside and 'Chunky' who had had half a bottle of free vodka, was being sick into a fire bucket. Henry patted his daughter's hand: 'I think that we should send it on to Mr Thomson don't you?'

Maisie leered horribly: 'At least we'll have a good excuse for not coming here!' She closed the briefcase carefully and, hand in hand, father and daughter walked down the gravel path, under the club chestnut tree and out into the street. As they walked back towards Maple Drive in the summer evening, Henry held his prize carefully. He had never liked Julian. He was never really able to like anyone who was good at tennis. But the man was certainly more bearable than most of the other members of the (British) Wimbledon Heights Tennis Club, Southfields. Henry smiled to himself sweetly and serenely as father and daughter walked up the front path of number fifty-two, and into the double-fronted house where all their feelings and opinions could be comfortably hidden from the outside world.

TINKER'S CURSE

Maurice Leitch

Maurice Leitch was born in County Antrim and educated in Belfast. He came to writing after working as a teacher in a county primary school for six years, and as a BBC Radio producer in Belfast. His novels include *The Liberty Lad*, *Poor Lazarus*, (which won the *Guardian* Fiction Prize), and *Burning Bridges*. He has recently completed a new novel.

TINKER'S CURSE was first broadcast on Radio 4, read by the author.

TINKER'S CURSE

I remember I had been sent into the town that afternoon for a message of some sort. But what was needed on my father's farm that day I can't recall, it happened such a long time ago. Anyway, details of that sort now seem unimportant after what did happen.

But I do remember meeting Sidney Hanlon on my way up Main Street and that we walked along together past the shops, past the nests of zinc buckets, the hay forks, hanging tools and bales of barbed wire displayed outside every grocer's doorway. The occasional car slipped past and the town-hall clock sleepily attacked the hour. Just another quiet, peaceful day in town, no different from any of the others in our little part of the world.

And then we saw the crowd. Just outside the barber's shop it was. A thick cluster of men all watching something or someone in their midst. Hanlon began to run.

'Come on!' he shouted. 'Mebbe it's a fight!' and I followed him.

There was a stranger in the centre of the crowd, and stripped to the waist, but he wasn't fighting. His challenge was of a different sort.

'Is there a sportsman in the crowd? Just one? Come, gentlemen, it's not every day you have the chance to see the like of such a fine performance.'

His eyes searched the faces. He wasn't a tall man but his body rippled with muscle. He had long matted hair, an earring and more tattoos than I would ever see in an entire lifetime. Two purple and green snakes struggled in writhing embrace up his left arm. Equally fearsome creatures, garlanded with inscriptions, patterned the rest of his torso.

As he continued to challenge the onlookers I still couldn't

make out what this 'fine performance' might be he was shouting about. The only clue was a heap of strong rope and an old brown blanket he had spread at his feet on the hot, dusty tarmacadam. But then he went on with his patter.

'Gentlemen, who will be the first to start the ball rollin'? Do I see a tanner? A shillin'? Come now, I promise you the spectacle of a lifetime. I guarantee, I repeat, I guarantee, to escape from these ropes in one minute or less. No, gentlemen, there's not the man livin' in any nook or corner of Ireland today who can tie up the great MacSweeney for any length of time. The knot was never invented that could keep him in captivity. As a wise man once remarked, the quickness of the hand ever deceives the eye – '

'An' sometimes blackens it!' interrupted a wag.

The crowd, the town's out-of-work to a man, who had been tempted across the road from Quinn's public house, laughed extravagantly. The tinker merely smiled, showing stained teeth.

'Ah, I see we have a philosopher in our midst.'

But he must not have appreciated the pleasantry for he glanced about for a victim to deflect the crowd's ridicule. And before I knew what was happening he was talking about Hanlon and me! I felt cold shudders run through me as I heard him say: 'By all the saints, I had no idea there was childer in the crowd. D'ye want to stunt your growth with the sight of what I'm about to perform? Come back when you've a little more hair on those puny chests, there's the good boys.'

Again the crowd guffawed.

Hanlon stuck out his tongue but didn't dare say anything – he didn't want a crack across the ear. I shrank quickly back to the fringes of the crowd. Then I felt a nudge in my ribs and Hanlon was beside me, unrepentant, and bold as brass.

'The church wall,' he pointed. 'Come, we'll have the fine grandstand view.'

We clambered up the wall that bounds the graveyard and found ourselves perches overlooking the crowd. The tinker had them really interested by this time. Across the street I could see the barber popping up his head from his work every now and then to peer out over his curtain and I could see a sixpence, two threepenny bits and a few coppers lying on the faded brown blanket.

Change continued to trickle in. A stranger – he looked like a tourist – threw down half-a-crown. At that point the tinker must have sensed there would be no more money. Already a few men were beginning to filter back across the road to the shadowy comforts of Quinn's.

'Very well, gentlemen!' he cried, clapping his hands. 'I'll begin. Now, is there a sport in the audience who'd like to have the rare honour of tyin' me up?'

He gazed impudently around him, feet apart, hands on his hips.

'Come, gentlemen, there's no need to be bashful. Your friends'll not think any the worse of ye for having failed miserably.'

No one moved.

In vain the tinker appealed for several minutes, first to the gathering at large and then finally to individuals. With no success.

And then he turned and stared straight up at the two of us on the wall. For the second time that afternoon shivers took hold of me.

'You up there! No, not you – the big one! How would you like the chance to prove yourself a proper man?'

Hanlon was down off the wall and over beside the tinker before you could say knife. Some of the crowd began to titter.

'Wud ye luk at the shrimp tryin' to lassoo the whale!' one man cried.

But, undeterred, Hanlon was darting around the broadly smiling tinker like a terrier around a bull – a quiescent bull – and to make it easier for him, he had stretched himself out on the blanket. The grin never left his face as he allowed the boy to roll him about from side to side, passively, like a sack of meal. Hanlon threw a couple of loops about his ankles, drew them tight and then tied the free end to his wrists. He stood back to admire his work.

It certainly looked all right. The knots were hard and firm, there wasn't a square foot of the man's tattooed body that wasn't criss-crossed with rope, but I knew that they wouldn't hold him for long. My father had taught me too much about knots for me not to see that.

The tinker seemed to realise it too, for he lay there lazily on his back, smiling, eyes closed, in a parody of sleep.

'I'm just goin' to stretch out here in the sun, until you've finished, boy. Don't rush yourself. Who knows you might even become famous in your own home town. Though I very much doubt it.'

He sighed contentedly as though at his ease on a feather mattress. The crowd laughed, enjoying the scene.

It was at that moment that I became involved. Looking back, I find it difficult to say what my true motives must have been. I suppose the taunts still stung. Perhaps it was the cheek of the man, a 'foreigner', in my eyes, by reason of his Southern accent. All I do know is that I began assisting Hanlon with his task and for once in his life my schoolmate kept his mouth shut.

Now one of my father's favourite knots about the farm and in the hayfield was a queer kind of running slip-knot. I say 'queer' because in all my travels I never once saw another man tie such a thing. It may very well have been my father's own invention – as I say, he had a taste for that sort of thing, more in keeping with a seafaring type than someone born and bred on a farm. Anyway that was the knot I used.

I took my time. The tinker was in no hurry either, he still had his eyes closed, and the crowd seemed content just to watch. Hanlon kept buzzing around as if he were doing all the work and when I had finished and slipped back to my old place on the wall he made no move to stop me.

I waited with beating heart to see what the tinker would do.

He began by feeling each knot and strand with infinite caution and respect. At times he barely moved, his eyes still shut as if he didn't want us to guess at what was going on in his mind. I watched fascinated.

The crowd had quietened. They waited. A minute passed.

The tinker continued to smile but the men watching were beginning to sense he was no longer in control of the situation.

A low muttering began. The veins on the tinker's forehead throbbed and sweat glistened on his body, his smile replaced by a look which clearly hinted at desperation. Finally he gave one convulsive struggle that lifted his trussed legs clear of the blanket and then he lay still, defeated. The crowd went quiet.

'All right! I'm bate!'

The shout sent a flock of starlings spraying from the church tower above my head.

'I admit it! Where's the boy? Where's the boy?'

Hanlon moved forward amid a great noise of contempt from the onlookers. I had never seen him so pale. His fingers trembled as he tore at the knots. I watched from my perch powerless to help as surely as if I had suddenly become part of the masonry and knowing with terrible certainty what was going to happen. I knew it. He couldn't unloose the knots. He gave me one piteous look but I was unable to budge. Finally the tinker thrust him away with a movement of his whole, coiled body. He cursed him in a low and terrible voice then lay back panting.

I saw one of the men in the crowd pull out a penknife. The tinker saw it too and yelled as the man bent towards him.

'No, damn you! Not my lovely ropes!'

The man hesitated and at that moment someone at the back of the crowd shouted out the one urgent word: 'Hannigan!' and all eyes turned in the direction of the barracks.

Constable Hannigan, face red and purposeful, had just strode through the gates. From the top of the wall I saw his glance take in the scene and then he was on the move. The crowd began to thin, deserting the tinker. His oaths rang out a second time but the crowd knew the constable only too well, a case of every man for himself, and the space before the barber's shop was suddenly empty, save for the desperate captive.

From where he lay on the ground the tinker couldn't see me high above him on the wall. But I could see him. I wanted to run away like all the rest, to have no part in it, but something held me back.

Hannigan was halfway up the street by now, his cheeks sweating with eagerness. He passed Uprichard's sweet shop and then, finally, I moved.

I knew I had to do it, no matter what happened. One thing was certain – the fat constable would never run.

My fingers touched the ropes and the tinker ceased struggling. He stayed stiff, unmoving, not speaking. I loosened the key knot and the rest came away at one sharp tug. That was my father's knot – child's play to untie, but only if you knew which one to loosen first. The ropes slid to the ground and the tinker stood up rubbing his cramped body.

Hannigan had stopped. He was staring into a drapery shop window with the utmost concentration.

Suddenly I became embarrassed standing there in the middle of the square like that. I was still aware of the tinker's presence, but he was no longer the forbidding figure he had been minutes before. I turned to go and his voice stopped me: 'Here, boy, this is for you'. He held out his hand.

Mechanically I took the half-crown and looked up at him. He was smiling but I felt uneasy as I turned away.

At the corner I looked back. He had gone, blanket, rope and trappings, as though he had never been.

I walked over the bridge still with that uneasy feeling; the terrible curses he had uttered earlier still in my head. I felt as though he had cursed me, too, in some strange, personal way, yet without uttering a single word.

My one desire was to rid myself of the memory of all that happened that afternoon. Before I crossed the bridge, I took the half-crown and with all my strength I hurled it far off up the river and watched it fall like a bright stone into the deepest water. Then I ran all the way home.

ACKNOWLEDGEMENTS

THE WIFE OF MY FRIEND © 1994 by Frederic Raphael
PERFECT STRANGERS © 1994 by Richard Burns
TAM O' SHANTER © 1993 by Donna Tartt
SUSPICION © 1994 by Deborah Moggach
I'LL SWING YOU ROUND BY THE
    TAIL © 1994 by Julia O'Faolain
KISS ME HARDY © 1993 by Beryl Bainbridge
THE PACT © 1994 by Joyce Carol Oates
LAST ONE OUT © 1994 by Steve Dixon
THE GHOST WRITER © 1993 by Julie Burchill
EDNA, BACK FROM AMERICA ©
    1994 by Clare Boylan
ALL OVER THE PLACE © 1994 by Michael Carson
RHINO-SKIN © 1994 by Moy McCrory
TRUE ROMANCE © 1994 by Caroline Forbes
STORMING THE BARRICADES ©
    1994 by Jonathan Treitel
LIVING HISTORY © 1994 by Martyn Read
RUN AND ASK DADDY IF HE HAS
    ANY MORE MONEY © 1993 by Fay Weldon
TRUMPET OF VICTORY © 1994 by Carl Tighe
SATURDAY IN THE 'SAC © 1994 by Alan Beard
THE RIGHT SET © 1994 by Nigel Williams
TINKER'S CURSE © 1994 by Maurice Leitch

DUNCAN MINSHULL

TELLING STORIES Volumes 1 and 2
The Best of BBC Radio's Recent Short Fiction

'A relaxing and enjoyable experience'
Literary Review

'A varied and distinctive collection'
Time Out

'There's a whole world in these stories'
Natalie Wheen on Kaleidoscope

Volume 1

A. L. Barker
Christopher Burns
Angela Carter
Jane Gardam
Christopher Hope
Deborah Moggach
Frederic Raphael
Dilys Rose
D. J. Taylor
Lynn Truss

Maeve Binchy
Michael Carson
Mary Flanagan
Romesh Gunesekera
John McGahern
Richard Nelson
Michele Roberts
Greg Snow
Jonathan Treitel

Volume 2

Stephen Amidon
Clare Boylan
Ronald Frame
Russell Hoban
Francis King
Penelope Lively
David Lodge
Peter Regent
Lawrence Scott
Gillian Tindall

Maeve Binchy
Irene Dische
Georgina Hammick
Angela Huth
Anne Leaton
Liz Lochhead
Shena Mackay
Frank Ronan
Greg Snow
Rose Tremain

CORONET BOOKS